COWBOYS
AND
FISHERMEN

968-HANC

COWBOYS
AND
FISHERMEN

Michael Hance

Library of Congress Number:		00-190394
ISBN #:	Hardcover	0-7388-1627-2
	Softcover	0-7388-1628-0

This is a work of fiction. Names, characters, places and incidents either are the product of the author's imagination or are used fictitiously, and any resemblance to any actual persons, living or dead, events, or locales is entirely coincidental.

This book was printed in the United States of America.

To order additional copies of this book, contact:
Xlibris Corporation
1-888-7-XLIBRIS
www.Xlibris.com
Orders@Xlibris.com

CONTENTS

CONTENTS

To my grandfather, "Peanuts" Davidson
and
To my father, Pete Hance

Also, to the women in our lives who make us strong.

CHAPTER 1

It was seven o'clock on a Sunday morning when he woke to the ringing of the telephone. He rubbed his face with both hands, squinting against the morning light that streamed in through the bedroom window, shielding his eyes with his forearm.

Out in the kitchen, his wife answered the phone. He could hear the murmur of her voice but not clearly enough to make out any words. After a few moments, he heard her place the receiver back in it's cradle. Her soft footsteps approached the bedroom door.

"Who was on the phone?" he asked from behind his arm.

"That was your sister."

Something in his wife's voice told him the news would not be good. He uncovered his eyes and looked at her. Her face was drained of colour and her dark eyes were bright with tears as she sat down on the edge of the bed and placed a warm hand on his thigh.

After a deep steadying breath, she told him.

"Your grandfather died last night."

The news ripped through his stomach and for a moment he forgot how to breathe. He stared blankly at the ceiling, unbelieving as he absorbed the sudden reality.

"How?" he was finally able to ask.

"He had a heart attack. He and your grandmother were at a dance and he went back to the trailer for a minute. When he didn't come back, she went looking for him. She found him on the bathroom floor. He was dead before the paramedics could get there."

"Did my sister say how everyone's doing?"

"Your mom's okay. She's upset, of course, but she's holding it together."

His mother was not the hysterical type, nor would she be overwhelmed by her grief. She would cry her tears of sadness, then dry her eyes and set about taking care of everyone else.

"Your sister seems to be doing okay, too."

His sister cried during reruns of *Little House on the Prairie*. He used to tease her that her kidneys were connected to her tear ducts. He also knew that, when necessary, she seemed able to draw on immense reserves of inner strength that allowed her to weather any crisis.

"Does my grandmother need anyone to go to her? How's she getting back?"

Just this year, his grandparents had decided to spend the winter in a Florida trailer park, shunning the cold and snow of the long Canadian winter.

"She's flying back tonight. They're flying your grandfather home on the same plane."

She searched her husband's face, noting the bunched muscle that jumped along his jaw.

"Are you okay?"

He nodded.

She leaned over and wrapped her arms around him.

He thought he should feel sad, but he didn't really. He couldn't cry. He just felt stunned. And lonely. And then strangely calm.

"My grandfather's dead," he said at last.

"I know."

* * *

"C'mon cowboy, the fish are waitin'."

A rough calloused hand shook his small foot and he propped himself up on his elbow and rubbed the sleep form his eyes with the back of his fist. He grinned up at his grandfather, showing the new space in his smile. Yesterday it had been filled with a wobbly baby tooth. It had lasted through dinner, only to fall out while eating his dessert pudding.

He was probing the empty socket with his tongue when he remembered the tooth fairy. He shot his hand under the pillow. Instead of finding the dime he had expected, his fingers closed around a long, thin cellophane wrapped box. He looked at the tear-drop shaped spoon inside; the red and white enamelled swirl, the silvered treble hook.

"A Dardevil," he cried.

"Best bass spoon ever," his grandfather answered. "That tooth fairy must know her way around a tackle box. C'mon, let's go."

He left the room as the boy shrugged out of his pyjamas and hurriedly pulled on his jeans and T-shirt. He stuck his feet into black canvas high tops and fumbled with the laces, his tongue curled over his upper lip with concentration. When they were tied, he pulled on a grey sweatshirt and capped off the ensemble with a black felt, flat-crowned cowboy hat with white cording around the brim. Thus attired, he hurried out of the cottage.

He found his grandfather on the dock loading the sixteen foot aluminum fishing boat.

"Can I carry your tackle box, Papa?" the boy asked,

"If you can handle her," the old man answered.

The boy grinned, flexing six year old biceps in his best muscleman pose. The tackle box, a heavy steel, three-tray model was in its usual spot on the boathouse floor. A water spider scurried off it's dull green side as the boy grasped the thick handle with both hands and hoisted it from the floor, his arms straight down in front of him, his back arched. The boy's own tackle box was a new plastic model, feather-light. But the old man insisted on using the old steel box, scarred and rusted, that he had bought back in '48. The boy loved the old box. To him it was magic. He would often sit cross-legged—"Indian-style" the old man called it—exploring the treasures inside. The scarred wooden muskie baits conjured images of monumental battles with fanged fish bigger even than the boy himself. Rubber-skirted Hula Poppers and pop-eyed Zara Spooks harkened to humid summer nights spent slapping mosquitoes and spincasting for smallmouth bass. Cardboard-backed packs of Eagle Claw snelled hooks and tubes of split-shot sinkers that made a "shooka shooka" sound when he rattled them next to his ear. Other names like Black Fury and Silver Fox, Swedish Pimple and Jitterbug and Rapala sounded as an angler's incantation that mingled deliciously with the odours of fish, dew worms, gasoline and wood smoke that rose from within.

The boy struggled to the side of the boat where the old man relieved him of the heavy box. The boy then handed down his own small black plastic container, after tucking his new spoon safely inside. His light blue fibreglass Algonquin rod and reel, a Christmas gift ("That Santa Claus must know his way around a fish", his grandfather had commented) already lay in the well of the boat, next to the old man's ancient cork-handled red Shakespeare.

"Prepare to cast off", the old man ordered.

"Aye, aye, Cap'n, sir."

The boy undid the knots in the mooring lines, a skill learned as a result of a rainy afternoon spent patiently imitating over and over the deft motions of his grandfather's hands, while the old man squeezed the bulb that drew fuel into the line connecting the sun-oranged gas can to the blue and white, nine-and-a-half horsepower Evinrude. He opened the choke, shifted to neutral and tugged at the pullcord. After three tries, the motor sputtered to life, breathing blue-grey smoke out over the water. The boy loved that sound and the pungent smell released by the little two-stroke motor filled him with a sense excitement and adventure.

"Hop in. Watch yourself, now. Careful", the old man fussed, knowing that if the boy fell in it would be himself who would catch hell.

He held the boat close to the dock; strong, blunt fingers gripping the rubber trailer tires that were nailed to the side of the floating structure to serve as fenders. The boy tossed the paynter into the boat and, steadying himself with a hand on the dew-covered gunwhale, stepped on board. His grandfather slipped the outboard into reverse and backed away from the dock while the boy settled onto the middle bench, an orange keyhole lifejacket under him to cushion the ride and another around his neck in case he fell overboard. ("You're mom worries. If it were up to me . . . well' you better wear one anyways").

The boat was moving forward now, its wake rolling away, yellow-green and white across the black surface of the water. The sun was rising, lemon-yellow in a clear blue sky, and was already warming the air.

The sweatshirt would soon come off. The wind created by the boat's movement tugged at the brim of the boy's cowboy hat and he tightened the string under his chin. He remembered too well the day this past spring when this hat's predecessor was gustily snatched from his head on the first boat ride of the season. The sodden hat was retrieved and taken back to the cottage where an attempt was made to dry it in the kitchen oven. That was how he discovered that cheap, wet felt combined with intense, dry heat resulted in a stiff, shrunken, misshapen mess. That unfortunate hat was replaced with the one he now wore on his head.

The motor lowered its voice as his grandfather throttled back. He eased the boat through a gap in a jam of driftwood and they entered a weed- and log-choked bay. There were no cottages here, only silent stands of spruce and cedar, mixed with a few white birch. Fallen trees in various stages of decay littered the rocky shoreline and lined the bottom of the bay where smallmouth bass lurked in the shadows, waiting for a meal to swim by.

The old man cut the motor and he and the boy traded seats. He fitted the long varnished oars into their locks and halted the forward drift of the boat. The two fishermen then collected their rods and opened their tackle boxes.

The old man, conscious of the weeds and the deadheads, selected a small Rapala. Its thin, torpedo body of silver and black balsa wood was fitted with a shallow diving lip, making it extremely manoeuvrable. In the hands of an experienced fisherman, it could be dropped into hiding spots and floated over snags. He tied the lure to his line and tightened the knotted monofiliment with his teeth.

The boy was busily tearing into the package that held his new Dardevil.

"Spoon's pretty heavy for this kind of cover", the old man cautioned.

"It'll be okay", the boy replied, doubting his own judgement even as he spoke.

"Suit yourself". *Can't tell him. He'll have to learn for himself. Stubborn little bugger, just like his father. Just like me.*

The boy attached the lure to his line with a small brass swivel snap, his young fingers that still occasionally fumbled over a shoestring as yet too untrained to tie complex clinches in fishing line.

The old man pulled on an oar, swinging the boat into position. He would fish off the port side as usual, out of habit as well as a superstition, although he would never admit to the latter. He cast out his line, the lure catching the sun on its silvery hide as it arced gracefully out over the water. The Rapala entered the bay almost without a sound. He began his retrieve, pulling and playing the minnow-shaped lure into likely hiding spots.

Off the starboard side, the boy prepared for his cast. He let about a foot of line dangle from the end of his rod, then depressed the thumb button on his reel, locking the line into place. Slowly, he raised the tip of the rod, letting the spoon fall behind his right shoulder. Taking a deep breath, his brow furrowing in concentration, he flung the rod tip forward, releasing the thumb button at the same time to open the bail. The heavy spoon unspooled line and drew it across the water until the Dardevil landed with a small plop. Shifting the rod to his left hand, he began reeling in line with his right. Through a quirk of comfort, he both casted and retrieved with the same hand.

The old man had watched the entire procedure out of the corner of his eye. *Pretty good cast*, he thought, allowing a small smile to tug at the corner of his mouth. It was then he realized he had been holding his breath.

The boy had reeled his new spoon back in about fifteen feet when he felt resistance. He stopped cranking and released the bail.

If a fish was testing the bait, the line would begin to let out. It didn't. The boy began to turn the handle again, slowly. The line tightened, bending the rod tip down a little. He tugged, tentatively at first, then a little more forcefully. The spoon's treble hook only bit more deeply into the log it had found on the bottom of the bay. *Spoon's pretty heavy for this kind of cover*, he heard his grandfather's warning repeat itself in his mind. He should have listened. What would the old man say? The boy glanced in his direction. The old man was just finishing a retrieve. The Rapala dripped jewels of water from its body. Its painted eye and red grinning mouth smiled mockingly back at the boy. The old man snapped his wrist and the lure was soaring back out over the water once more. The boy thought of his own brand new spoon imbedded in a spruce log a dozen feet below the surface.

On the shore, a mink foraging for crayfish stopped and looked out at the boat. The boy stared into the water. A heron stilted through the shallows, trying to spear its breakfast. A broad-winged hawk spiralled away from its perch amongst the spruce, stretching its muscles in the warmth of the morning sun. The boy looked away, his eyes falling on a deadhead stump. A painted turtle looked back.

"Somethin' the matter?" His grandfather's voice came softly.

"Snagged."

"Lemme see", the old man said. *Told you so*, he thought. A couple of sharp tugs told him the spoon was down there to stay.

"Gonna have to cut 'er loose", he said. *Ol' Tooth Fairy's out a buck and a quarter*, he thought.

The boy sat slumped on the bench. He stared at the point where his line disappeared into the water, his throat tight as he fought back tears of humiliation at his stupidity and the loss of his new, prized spoon. Cowboys don't cry. Neither do fishermen.

The old man watched the boy intently. *Hell, it's only a lure*, he thought. *I've lost dozens of 'em, for chrissake*. Then something inside him shifted and he shared the boy's sorrow.

"I do hate to lose a good piece of tackle, though", the old man said. He propped his rod across his seat. Gripping the oars, he rowed to the spot where the lure lay trapped. Looking down into the tannin-stained water, he could make out a dull glint of metal. *Not more'n ten, fifteen foot deep. What the hell, nice mornin' for a swim.*

"Well, let's see what we can do about gettin' that Dardevil back", the old man said.

He pulled his bare feet out of his laceless, paint-spattered work shoes and slipped out of his red corduroy shirt. Unbuckling his belt, he removed his baggy green work pants and stood there in his raggedy white jockeys. "Be right back", he said and shallow-dove off the back of the boat.

He quickly kicked his way down to the snag, sliding the line through his fingers to guide his descent. Feeling for the lure, he held tight to the log with his left hand while, with his right, he worked the hooks free from the wood. Fifteen seconds had elapsed and already he was aware of the lack of oxygen. *Must be getting old*, he chided himself.

The hooks were free now. He hung motionless to allow his feet to sink beneath him then kicked toward the surface. His left foot caught on the log and his push moved him only a couple of feet upwards. Almost thirty seconds had passed since had entered the water. As he gathered himself for another kick, he fought down a rising panic. One last kick, awkward with desperation, finally carried him to the surface. He felt a rush of relief as he gulped fresh air. He raised his arm triumphantly above his head, the recovered spoon dangling from his hand like the catch of the day.

"Got it."

"Gee, Papa! I bet you could swim across the *whole* lake under water", the boy said, his voice filled with awe.

"No problem", he answered. *Goddamned Tooth Fairy*, he thought. He hauled himself back aboard and towelled off with his shirt. He quickly dressed, hanging his soaking undershorts on the tiller of the outboard to dry. He then tied a single hook onto the boy's line and Texas-rigged a plastic grub, driving the point of the hook back through the soft body, rendering it weed- and snag-proof. The boy then proceeded to outfish him, three keepers to one.

"Thirsty?". The old man had already decided he was.

"Yup, I sure am," the boy answered in his best six-year old barroom drawl.

The old man reached past the boy and grabbed their drinks from where they sat on the transom support in the shad of the motor. He rummaged in his tackle box for an opener. Holding a can of root beer out over the side of the boat, he punched two holes in the top. Foam spilled over his hand and he rinsed it off in the lake. He handed the can to the boy. He then picked up his bottle of Black Label and, using the reverse end of the opener, snapped the cap off the stubby brown bottle. They toasted each other.

"Here's looking up yer old address," the old man said.

"Here's mud in yer eye," replied the boy.

They both grinned.

"I drove a herd of cattle down
from old Nebraska way . . . ."
The old man sand soft and low as he worked the lure back towards the boat.

"That's how I cam to be in
the state of I-O-Way . . . ."
Beside fishing, one of his greatest passions was the cowboy way.

"I met a girl in I-O-Way
her eyes were big and blue . . . ."
He loved to sing their songs. He knew hundreds of them.

"I asked her what her name was
and she said Sioux City Sue"
He sometimes still imagined himself as a cowboy. The rocking of the boat became the rocking of the saddle.

"Sioux City Sue, Sioux, City Sue
hair of gold and eyes of blue.
I'd swap my horse and my dog for you"

A tug on the line brought him back to reality.
The boy was smiling. He loved to hear his grandfather sing.

"Four on the stringer," the old man said. "Let's head for home.
Trade 'ya seats."

They hooked their lures to the lower guides of their rods and
laid them in the bottom of the boat. The boy settled onto the life
jacket and watched as his grandfather started up the outboard.

"Papa . . . could I drive the boat?"

"I guess so, come on back . . . easy now."

The old man straddled the rear bench and the boy settled in
between his knees and placed his hand on the tiller. The smooth
plastic throttle control vibrated under his touch and as he twisted
the grip, the boat surged forward. His grandfather's hand rested
behind his, right where the two spare shear pins were fastened to
the arm with a twist of black electrical tape.

"Papa?"

"Mmm?"

"I'm gonna be a cowboy when I grow up!"

"Good," said the old man. *Not for a few more years, I hope,* he
thought. The boy leaned back and put his head on the man's chest.

The boy was six, the old man was forty seven.

CHAPTER 2

There was a chill rising from the ground that the early morning March sun hadn't yet chased from the air. Large patches of winter-browned grass showed through the remaining snow, only the low and shady areas retained the white cloak of winter. The granular, grit-filled snowbanks that the season's shovelling had piled beside the pavement and the sidewalks were being eaten away more and more each day. Already trickles of meltwater stained the gutters dark grey.

Sleds and toboggans had given way to bicycles and skateboards. On each street, road hockey players were shedding mitts and toques and scarves. Some brave souls, safely out of their mothers' sights, had even shed their coats to play in shirtsleeves.

Birdsong filled the air; robins just returned from vacation.

The young man stepped outside and breathed deeply the earth-scented air. Even the warm promise of spring failed to lighten the weight of loss that pressed down upon him.

Behind him, the screen door creaked open, then closed with a hiss. The young man's wife moved beside him, taking his arm. She looked up at him, trying to gauge how well he was reacting to the situation. He felt her studying him and gave her a slight, though humourless smile, an attempt to reassure her that he would be alright.

Together they walked to the car.

* * *

The cottage door opened and a blast of dry, frigid air swept in low along the floor. The old man stomped inside, his unzipped, felt-lined boots clumping on the linoleum. He carried a load of firewood in the crook of his left arm.

"Whew, that's cold out there . . . freeze a witch's brass monkey."

He dumped the wood next to the metal woodstove, then squatted down and began feeding the flames.

The boy lay on the floor, a pad of paper and a scattering of pencil crayons on the rug in front of him. He carefully shaded with a crimson Laurentian, putting the finishing touches on his drawing of a hard-charging New York Ranger.

His father sat in the chair beside where the boy lay, waiting for the commercial on the black and white portable to end and the game to begin.

The Maple Leafs were on a western road swing, playing the night before in Oakland and the next afternoon in Los Angeles. Therefore "Hockey Night in Canada" was broadcasting nationally the Canadiens and the Bruins from the Montreal Forum.

The old man drew the firescreen closed, rose and brushed bark chips from his blue plaid flannel shirt. He crossed the room and settled on the couch.

The game flickered onto the screen and soon Boston had jumped out to a quick lead, Wayne Cashman shovelling in a Phil Esposito rebound.

Danny Gallivan described "cannonading drives" followed by "scintillating saves."

At the halfway mark of the first period Boston went up 2-0 when Johnny Bucyk converted a beautiful pass from Don Marcotte.

Dick Irvin began reminiscing about a Habs-Bruins game from 1950-something when his dad had stood behind the Montreal bench.

The old man cast a sly sidewards glance at his son-in-law. *Time to get out the needle.*

"Dick's right", he said. "The Hab's haven't been the same since Rocket Richard retired."

Here it comes, the boy muttered to himself.

"Yup! Rocket Richard! The best ever!". Another sideways glance. Nothing. Tough fishing tonight.

"Hull, Beliveau, Morenz, Harvey, Schmidt . . . ". Jigging, jigging. His son-in-law's jaw muscles were working. Time to set the hook.

". . . Howe."

"Richard couldn't carry Howe's skates!".

The old man smirked. The boy groaned. His father was a big fan of the Detroit Red Wings in general and the great Gordie Howe in particular, following his career from the time the man was a boy himself.

The old man, while he admired the explosive Rocket, was never a real Richard fan. He didn't really follow or even understand the game, at least not the way his son-in-law and grandson did. His sport was teasing, needling. Shit-disturbing.

". . . Maybe from the blueline in Richard was great, but Howe could do it all; skate, shoot, score, pass, check, fight . . . "

"Never got fifty goals. The Rocket got fifty. And he did it in fifty games, too."

His son-in-law always swore he wouldn't rise to the old man's bait. He just couldn't help himself.

"How many Art Rosses did Richard win? None! Howe's got six. Six Hart trophies, too."

Can't argue with that, the old man admitted to himself.. *Time to get some help.*

"Let's let the boy decide", he said. "Who's the best hockey player of all time; Maurice 'The Rocket' Richard or Gordie Howe?"

Why me?, thought the boy. He had been raised on stories of Gordie Howe and truly admired the right-winger's all-around greatness. His dad would like it if the boy sided with him.

But the boy was also definitely his grandfather's grandson. He loved to tease and the old man would be beside himself with devilish glee to have the boy as an ally in this debate.

The boy decided that the time had come to stand up and be

counted, to declare his opinion and let the chips fall where they may. He cast his own sideways glances.

His father's eyes spoke to him. *You know Howe is the best. You know it.*

His grandfather's poker face seemed disinterested, only the mischievous glint in his eyes letting his feelings known. *Richard, Richard, Richard, Richard! C'mon boy, I've got your dad to the side of the boat, now help me land him! Say Richard!*

The boy looked at the two men again, then turned his attention back to the T.V. His face twitched as he fought down a smile.

"Bobby Orr's got 'em both beat", he declared then turned his attention back to the game.

The two men looked at each other and nodded, grinning foolishly as they acknowledged mutual defeat while at the same time sharing mutual pride in the boy's burgeoning independence.

The next morning, the boy awoke in the pale light of an early sunrise. Chickadees were already busy outside, arguing with a blue jay over breakfast. From the kitchen came the smell of bacon and snatches of low whistling; "Red River Valley". The boy pulled his jeans over his longjohns and struggled a fisherman-knit sweater over his head. He yawned and combed his hair with his fingers. The whistling turned to singing and he followed the sound out of the bedroom, down the hall and into the kitchen.

"From this valley they say you are leaving,
We will miss your bright eyes and sweet smile.
For they say you are taking the sunshine,
That had brightened our lives for awhile."

The boy grinned at the sound of the singing. "Morning", he said.

"Mornin' pardner", his grandfather replied. "You the only one up?"

"Just you and me."

The old man stood in front of a skillet full of sizzling bacon, one hand on his hip, the other holding a fork that was his favourite

cooking utensil, along with a long fileting knife, honed razor-sharp
and needle-thin and kept safely in an oiled leather sheath. A single
button held his flannel shirt closed over his belly. Beside him on
the counter sat a dozen eggs, a pound of bacon, a loaf of bread, and
a plate of fresh perch fillets, caught the day before.

"You wanna scramble up some eggs for me?", the old man
asked.

The boy got down a big mixing bowl and began cracking eggs
into it, being careful not to include any shell fragments.

"How many should I do?"

"Might as well do 'em all. Just leave me a couple for the fish."

The old man lifted the bacon out of the skillet and layered it
on a plate, each row separated from the one on top by a folded
piece of paper towel. He then reloaded the skillet and reached for
his 'juice'; rye and water, two ice cubes. He took a sip and then got
from the cupboard two small bowls. Into one bowl, he broke two
eggs and vigorously beat them with his fork. He poured cornflakes
into the second bowl and crushed them with strong fingers. The
perch were then dipped into the eggs and rolled in the corn flake
crumbs. These would soon be fried to golden perfection in the
bacon grease now accumulating in the skillet.

The boy's mother sleepily entered the kitchen and began feeding bread into the antique drop-sided toaster. His sister and his
grandmother emerged from their rooms and started to set the table.

The boy poured milk into the bowl of eggs and began beating
the mixture with a fork. He whisked them together until a froth
formed on top, then spooned them onto the buttered surface of an
electric griddle. He immediately began worrying the eggs with a
spatula.

The old man and the boy moved about one another in the
cramped space between counter top and stove with an unrehearsed
elegance, avoiding collisions with unspoken directions.

The eggs were done just as his grandfather lifted the last piece
of fish from the skillet.

"I'll go get dad up", the boy said.

"Naw, let him sleep. He gets up early all week.". The old man knew his son-in-law rose at 5:30 a.m. all week to go to his job on the assembly line, building cars eight hours a day. He needed his weekend rest to recharge his batteries. The old man placed some fish and a few strips of bacon on a plate and set it in the oven. It would still be warm when his son-in-law rolled out of bed an hour later.

The old man's daughter brought her future husband home when the young lovers were both fifteen. Her father immediately resented the fact he was now competing with this handsome, head-strong young man for his daughter's attention. The boyfriend hated the way he felt constantly compelled to measure up to his best girl's stubborn old father. It was a relationship with only one thing in common: they both fiercely loved the same young girl.

To be near his true love, the young man tagged along on family outings. He learned to fish and came to actually like the outdoors, enjoying the fall the best, the winter least.

To be near his daughter, the old man accompanied her to watch her athletic young hero guard first base or skate up and down right wing. He learned to love baseball and, years later, would once again freeze his ass off watching his grandson patrol the right side of the hockey rink.

One fine day, the old man heard his daughter say those dreaded words; "Dad, we're getting married. In June."

His first thought was *They're too young. It won't last.* Then he looked at them; her face eager and hopeful; his showing a strength and determination the old man found oddly comforting.

He looked at the way they held hands, their fingers laced together in an unbreakable bond that would keep them together through any storm.

The old man suddenly realized that, if he had to lose his daughter, he was glad it was to this young man.

The wedding day went by in a whirl of tight collars and taffeta dresses, handshakes and best wishes, champagne and flash bulbs.

The bride was radiant, the groom nervous and uncomfortable in the rented tux. The old man shook a hundred hands and danced with his wife, thinking that she was more beautiful today then she was twenty two years ago when they waltzed at their own wedding.

Later that night, as he sat wondering how in the hell confetti managed to get into his undershorts, he felt that he had entered another stage in his life. As his wife lay down next to him, her wedding-day bouffant wrapped protectively in toilet paper, he had a thought.

"Maybe we should get a smaller place. Maybe an apartment . . . and a cottage."

"We'll talk about it in the morning." his wife yawned.

"Okay" he replied. "In the morning."

Nine months and five days later, the young couple made him a grandfather.

The next year he purchased the cottage lot. On the way back to the city, he stopped at a Canadian Tire and bought his grandson a fishing rod.

"Well, I'm headin' out to the fishin' hut for an hour or two. Anybody wanna come?" The old man was shrugging into his snowmobile suit.

The boy was grabbing for his hockey jacket before the question was even finished.

His mother took an immediate interest

"Put a sweater on under your coat. Have you got your snowpants on? Your scarf?"

The boy looked up from tying the laces of his rubber mukluks.

"Yes, Mom." He looked up at his grandfather. They rolled their eyes and grinned at one another.

"You comin' Dad?" the boy asked his father.

His dad was standing at the window, a second cup of coffee steaming in his hand. He was gazing out at the wind-blown snow that covered the lake, the drifts corrugated into frozen waves. The promising sunrise had been replaced by dark clouds that were already sending large flakes of snow diagonally to the ground. The dull grey light put him in the mood for a nap by the fire.

"Naw, I'm gonna stay here. You go on with your Papa. Besides, I wanna get an early start home in case the weather turns bad."

The boy's parents liked to head home by mid-afternoon, beating the traffic and the early winter darkness. The boy would wait and go home with his grandparents. They usually spent Sunday night at the cottage, rising in the pre-dawn to drive to the city, arriving in time for his grandfather to have breakfast before going to work.

"Okay, Dad. See ya." The boy went out the door.

"Good luck fishin'" his father called after him. *Who the hell would go out in weather like this to sit and stare down a hole in the ice?* he thought to himself. His father-in-law for one. And his son.

When the boy's father was born, his own father had been over forty. This age difference, and his father's poor health brought on by years of heavy drinking, had resulted in a very cool relationship between them. Of his seven older siblings, one had run away, three had married and one was in prison by the time he was old enough to remember them. His two sisters still living at home spent as much time away as possible. His mother was demanding and distant, worn down from giving birth to eight children, the first coming only ten months after she became a sixteen year old bride. Three more babies had come over the next four years. A life spent raising a large family on a paycheck often depleted by her husband's habitual visits to the beer parlour, had left her tired and overburdened.

When the boy's father first met his future in-laws, he had entered a whole new world, his life suddenly included experiences he had never known before. The old man and his wife took an interest in him that his own parents had never shown. The feelings he felt for them were foreign and, at times, disturbing. Years later, he would realize that, while he was falling love with their daughter, he was also falling in love with them.

His girlfriend's mother doted on him, fussing over him, offering seconds then thirds and fourths whenever he stayed for dinner. The old man taught him how to build a house and how to drive an outboard motor. He taught, by example, how to treat a family, how to be a man. They often ran afoul of the other, butting heads like elk, the young buck rebelling against the dominant place held by the old bull; the old bull doing his damnedest to hold the top spot for a little while longer. It wasn't until his own boy was in his teens that the man would recognize these struggles as those which normally occur between a father and a son.

They constantly sought each other's respect and, although neither would admit, each was slightly jealous of the other.

The boy reminded the old man of his son-in-law. The son-in-law saw a lot of the old man in the boy. Neither was unhappy with the resemblance.

The old man knelt on the red vinyl seat of the Evinrude snow cruiser. It was a big 1969-model and it growled to life with a single pull of the starter cord. The boy finished buckling on his helmet and climbed aboard his grandmother's '71 'Rude and thumbed the electric start. He rode in imitation of his grandfather; left foot on the running board, right knee on the seat, better to allow his legs and hips absorb the shock of the uneven ground. They pulled out of the side yard and headed down the hill toward the lake. The snow was falling faster now, the wind picking up.

After a ten minute ride, they pulled up in front of the red-painted fish hut, it's chipboard sides showing silvery patches where the elements had taken their toll. A piece of old stove pipe jutted above grey asphalt shingles. Snow was banked high against the six-by-sixes that formed the base of the shed. These also served as runners, necessary for towing the hut out on the lake as soon as the ice would support it's weight and hauled back in again when spring began to rot the ice. (Most years the water would rise over their boot tops as the old man and the boy struggled to drag it back to shore, the snowmobiles bogging down in the slush. "Gonna bring this son-of-a-bitch in earlier next year," the old man would always say.)

The boy watched two ravens brave the headwind as they flapped over the dark spruce and cedars on shore.

The old man opened the padlock on the door and flipped the latch. Kicking away a snow drift, he pulled open the door and the two fishermen went inside.

The boy unshuttered the small window and in the weak light the old man lit the small oil stove, tinkering with the valve until he achieved a satisfactory fuel-to-air mixture. He stood and slipped off the top of his snowmobile suit. The boy, in a reckless act of rebellion against his mother, removed his scarf.

The fishing holes that had been augured in the ice were exposed by removing two plywood trapdoors. The old man chopped at the skim of ice that had formed on top of the holes with an old yellow screwdriver then ladled out the slush with a long-handled sieve.

As he settled back on the flip-down bench padded with a flowered cushion, "liberated" as the old man would put it, from his wife's chaise lounge, the boy handed over his grandfather's rod, already baited with a Swedish Pimple jig. The lure was sweetened with a salt minnow, an atrophied shiner encrusted with rock salt, it's juices causing the whole mess to become a sickly ochre colour. Perch found them irresistible.

The old man used a rod made from eighteen inches of fibreglass rod tip salvaged from a brand new Fenwick he had slammed in the trunk of his car. He had epoxied this into a short piece of dowel to serve as a handle and secured an old spinning reel to it with a pair of pipe clamps.

The boy was using his favourite, a two foot length of steel rod fitted with orange plastic guides, the loose middle guide receiving additional support with a few twists of electrical tape. A simple baitcasting reel, also orange, also plastic, worked with surprising smoothness and strength. The handle was what made the rod so special. An orange plastic fish, with exaggerated scales, bulging eyes and a demented grin. White adhesive tape wrapped around it's middle made it look like the fish had suffered some sort of terrible back injury. The tape, combined with the insane expression, gave the impression that the fish enjoyed it's injury in some twisted masochistic way. The boy had had the rod for a long time. His grandfather had bought it for him when he was only a year old.

The pair dropped their lines down the holes and, hunched forward, with elbows on knees, began rhythmically jigging the lures up and down, up and down. Outside the wind hushed around the corners of the small hut.

"The wind's really picking up out there."

The old man had just come in from relieving himself ("Got to see a man about a horse" he had announced). A gust of Arctic wind had spoiled his attempted signature.

"Let's have a bite to eat and, if we don't catch anything by the time we're done, we can head back."

All they had to show for two hours work were three small perch now stiffening in the snow outside the hut.

The old man reached into his snow suit pocket and drew out two sandwiches wrapped neatly in waxed paper. He tossed one to the boy and then unfolded the covering from his own. Fresh white bread stuffed with sliced cheese and a thick slab of Spanish onion. He took up one half and held it in his hand, an index finger extending along the crusts edge. He took a huge, crunching bite and savoured the onion's hot sweet taste.

The boy looked on with revulsion. Cheese and onion! His ten-year-old palette could not understand how anyone could eat such a concoction, let alone enjoy it. He unwrapped his own sandwich and peaked between the bread. Aah! Now here was a sandwich truly worthy of eating. Tuna fish and ketchup.

The boy had almost finished his sandwich when he felt the first tappings on the line. He set the bread on his knee and gripped the rod in anticipation. Although he had yet to feel any weight, somehow he knew this was not another little perch. He waited, and when the tapping became a tug, he jerked the tip of the rod high, driving the treble hook deep into the jaw of his unknown prey. The fish immediately reacted, heading for deep water with such force that the rod was almost torn from the boy's trembling hands.

The old man quickly reeled in so as not to entangle his line with the boy's.

The boy, meanwhile, was fighting to control the situation. His sandwich had fallen from his lap, bounced once and disappeared down the hole, leaving no trace save for a few flakes of tuna and smear of ketchup on the toe of his left boot. He cranked the small reel spasmodically as the fish twisted and turned, furiously fighting for his freedom. His grandfather crouched down, running a bare hand around the hole, smoothing any spots that might fray the boy's line. He, too, realized the youngster had tied into something out of the ordinary.

The boy continued to fight the big fish, his arms pumping the rod in order to gain line. He could feel his back growing damp with the exertion, his jaw working fiercely as he ground his teeth. Cramping fingers held the rod and reel in a talon grip, knuckles white. His thin body was rigid with tension and it rocked back and forth, alternately pulling up then leaning forward as he gathered line.

His grandfather stayed hunched over the hole, his own body tensed and twitching as he fought an imaginary, though equally big, fish, his murmured advice providing a running commentary on the battle.

"Don't give him any slack . . . keep the tip up . . . that's it . . . work him . . . work him . . . come on up, you bugger, let's see ya' . . . reel in, now, reel in . . . good, good . . . he's comin' . . ."

The boy could now feel the big fish tiring. He was winning

back more slack with each pull now. The line, where it entered the water, was a frenzy of motion around the hole as the fish desperately sought to avoid the disk of light coming from above.

He felt the fish bumping the underside of the ice. His grandfather grabbed the line in his hand and guided the fish up through the hole.

"Well now, didn't think there were any lake trout left in these waters", the old man exclaimed as the big fish flopped onto the wooden floor of the hut. "Nice one, too. Seven, maybe eight pounds."

The boy was staring, his mouth open. "I've never caught a fish that big in my whole life" he breathed.

"It's a nice one, all right", the old man agreed. "What 'ya wanna do with him?"

"Whaddya mean?"

"Well, we could stuff and hang him up, or we could eat him. Never really cared for the taste of trout myself, though. One thing's for sure; this old boy's been hidin' in the lake for a long time to get that big. You know, I wouldn't be surprised if he was the last trout left in this lake."

The old man looked at the boy. The boy looked at the fish.

"I never really liked the taste of trout, either," he said finally. The boy took the fish from his grandfather and cradled it in his arms. He knelt and slipped it back through the ice. With a flick of it's tail, the big fish was gone.

He looked up at his grandfather's face, searching for comment on what he had done.

Beside him the old man's bottom lip pouted out from a crooked smile. He nodded his head approvingly.

The threatening storm had turned into nothing more than a snow squall, thick flakes driven sideways by a hard wind that reduced the lines of his grandfather's snowmobile up ahead to a shadow, the taillight a pink blur leading the boy across the ice. The wind that had brought the snow was already rending ragged blue tears in the overcast. The sleds bounced over the hard-packed surface of the frozen lake, heading for the far shoreline and the shelter of the trees.

They ran the machines up on the shore and wended their way through the woods. The snow was letting up a little and the wind was blocked by the cedars that grew along all around. As they rode deeper into the forest, the scenery grew almost surreal. Limbs bent under the weight of the snow, forming an archway of thick, white lace over the trail and the drifts on either side marked the passing of deer, rabbit, fox and bobcat. The old man slowed his machine and brought the boy to a stop with his best "wagons halt" hand signal. A mittened hand directed the boy's attention to a ruffed grouse plowing it's way up a nearby embankment toward the cover of a dead fallen spruce.

The wind which had driven the snow with such fury now began to scatter the cloud cover and the sun showed weakly through the overcast. The day grew colder with the clearing air. The two snowmobilers found the road and whipped along it towards the cottage.

The boy's parents were loading their car to go home when he and his grandfather pulled up to the cottage. His grandmother held the door as his sister came out, loaded down with the flowered red suitcase in one hand, and her yellow haired companion, Mrs. Beasley, in the other.

"You think they'll believe us about the fish , Papa?" the boy asked.

"I doubt 'er. Fishermen have been known to exaggerate."

"In that case," said the boy with a nudge, "let's make it a twelve pounder."

They laughed together in conspiracy.

By nightfall, the sky had cleared completely and bright white stars shone down. The three-quarter moon rode high and brilliant creating a landscape of blue and silver.

The boy and the old man had just run the snowmobiles into

the boat house where they would hibernate through the week, protected from the elements, safely out of sight of joyriders. As they walked back to the cottage, the snow squeaked and crunched beneath their boots and their breath rose frostily in the brittle night air. The branches overhead cast a web of shadows upon the ground.

"Papa?"

"Hmm?"

"Was it right to let the fish go?"

"I think so."

"Papa?"

"Hmm?"

"It was a good fish, wasn't it?"

The old man draped his arm across the boy's slender shoulders. "It was a helluva good fish," he said.

CHAPTER 3

When the young man and his wife entered the kitchen, his mother was sitting at the table, a cup of tea going cold in front of her. He swollen, red rimmed eyes were dry now. She'd had her cry and was now gathering the strength she knew would be needed when her own mother flew in that night.

His father sat at the other end of the table, his face a mask of calm efficiency. He could always be counted on in a crisis and the young man tried always to follow his father's lead in these situations. A pad of paper lay on the table, matters that needed to be taken care of were listed in his father's purposeful block capitals.

His sister, home from university, bustled about the kitchen, tidying up messes that weren't there. His wife immediately set about helping her, wiping away non-existent crumbs with a damp cloth.

The morning sun filled the kitchen, the light only slightly diffused by the pale yellow curtains. The oaken cupboards glowed golden brown.

He sat down at the place that was his before he married and moved away and together they began to plan the days ahead.

* * *

The warm sun of early April filtered down through the trees and battled with the chill morning air. The sweet, acrid scent of wood smoke mingled with the odours of wet earth and fresh cedar. The old man and the boy walked slowly down the road, savouring both the smells and each other's company. The sandy, gritty soil crunched under their steps.

The old man wore his favourite green work pants tucked into grey wool socks. A blue and black check wool jacket covered a faded burgundy sweatshirt. His feet were protected from the spring mud by green rubber hunting boots, insulated with insoles of thick cork. The yellow laces were wrapped twice around his ankles and tied. The boy beside him wore identical boots, his Levi's stuffed into the tops. A grey hooded sweatshirt was worn under the boy's pride and joy, a royal blue nylon hockey jacket crested with an old English "C" of the Cedardale Church Hockey Club, proud novice champions of the past season. A blue number nine superimposed over white crossed hockey sticks adorned the left sleeve. Blue and white striped knit inserts marked the shoulders and matched the stand-up collar. The boy now wore it with the white domed snaps undone, feeling the warmth of the spring sun on his small chest.

He sauntered along in imitation of his grandfather, shoulders hanging relaxed, hands deep in his pockets. Gangly bowed legs and a slight backward lean created the casual swagger of someone comfortable with his own movements. A sailor on a rolling deck maybe. Or a cowboy strolling toward the bunk house.

As they approached the dam that controlled the outflow of the lake, they left the road and leaped over the ditch where spring run-off bubbled brightly in tiny rivulets. Matted winter grass showed the higher levels of the season's meltwater.

They followed a narrow dirt trail to the edge of the dam, then stepped out onto the crumbling concrete structure, gripping the iron pipe of the handrail. Making their way to the middle they looked straight down on the spillway. Water frothed white and yellow over the timbers that controlled the lake level as well as that of the creek that flowed from it. The boy and the old man both spit into the churning water below the dam. "For luck," the old man said.

They climbed back down off the dam and continued along the trail as it followed the creek. A kingfisher darted across the water, it's white underbelly and rust throat stripe contrasting beautifully with the slate-blue wings and back, its large crested head and needle-like bill swivelling as the bird searched the water for a meal.

Downstream, the creek was littered with wooden track sections and rusting iron pushcarts abandoned after a short-lived attempt at establishing a uranium mine here back in the 'twenties. They soon came to the mine itself with it's heavy timbered adit. A chill breeze always blew out of the opening, filling the boy as it always did with a sense of mysterious foreboding. He and the old man had once explored the shaft for a distance of more than a hundred yards. In the weak illumination of a small flashlight, they found rusted tin cans, an old lantern and the remains of a block and tackle. His courage ran out at the same time the flashlight batteries did and he strongly suggested a return to the outside. The old man didn't argue. Feeling their way back along dripping rock walls, they finally stumbled out into the sunshine. With bravado betrayed by sheepish grins, they vowed to return one day with better lighting. Somehow, they both knew they never would.

Soon after they had passed the mine, the trail petered out and they stepped off into the bush. They moved now with their toes turned in slightly so as not to snag in the underbrush, an old Indian trick passed from grandfather to grandson. Granular snow still lay in the shadows, white scabs that contrasted icily with the deep rust carpet of fallen spruce and pine needles.

Climbing a low hill they entered a hardwood thicket. Overhead, buds on branches of sugar maple, oak and beech had burst open, sticky amber husks no longer able to contain the unfurling green growth within. Around the trunks, yellow crocuses grew, nourished by the warmth of the spring sun and the rich layer of composting leaf mould.

A single old growth white pine, windblown and lightning scarred, stood in the middle of the woods. Pellets of fur and bone on the ground beneath its broad boughs betrayed the winter roost of a great horned owl. They paused briefly to inspect their find before moving off once more in search of new treasures.

By mid-afternoon, they were circling an old beaver pond, already half drained, it's bottom swampy and choked with bulrushes and sedge grass. The beaver lodge still stood in the centre, and untidy mound of silvery gray sticks. Stumps of drowned trees spiked the old pond. New young aspen and birch grew around its perimeter. Wide girdles of bark had been stripped from their trunks by deer desperate for forage during the deep snows of winter.

The pond had been abandoned years ago. It had been started one spring by a pair of beavers who came upon the spot and decided to settle down. Here they had been content. A small stream had been dammed and the bottom land had filled quickly. They worked steadily throughout the summer months, cutting and trimming trees, their orange-yellow teeth gnawing through trunk and limb. Soon the lodge was finished, it's nesting den warm and dry. A ready food supply was stored beneath the surface of the pond.

She was heavy with young when the wolves came. They found a chink in the den and dragged her out, flipping her constantly from behind, wary of her sharp teeth. She quickly tired and the big predators moved in for the kill.

He had been able to escape and he floated out of reach, watching, helpless with rage and fear. He knew any attempt to come to her rescue would be futile. After the wolves had gone, he still sat for a long while, immobilized by his grief and shock.

He tried returning to the den. Her scent was everywhere yet only served to remind him that she was gone. Finally, he shambled away.

"Did I ever show you the Hermit's house?"

They had been following the small stream for a mile or so, crossing and recrossing it, finding the path of least resistance, much in the manner of the stream itself.

"What's the Hermit's house?" the boy asked.

"C'mon, I'll show ya"

His grandfather headed away from the stream and the boy quickly followed him. After walking about a hundred feet into the forest, they broke into a clearing. Oak leaves covered the ground in a thick, decaying mat. At the back of the clearing, a small cabin sagged toward the earth, its roof coated with moss and lichen. The only window was a black opening beside the door, its four glass panes missing, falling out as the putty dried and let go. The plank door hung open, its leather hinges cracked and splitting. Holes showed in the walls where the moss chinking had worked loose. A rose bush climbed wild and thorny up the side of the building.

The old man led the way inside. Cracked and curled linoleum covered a rough-sawn plank floor. The whole building was one room, measuring about twelve feet square. Light streamed through a dozen places in the roof. A ragged flour sack that had served as a curtain hung limp form one last nail in the window frame. A steel drum converted into a wood stove stood in the corner, rust and soot covering its sides, and an iron bed was pushed against the back wall, it's mattress water-stained and mildewed, home to a family of deer mice. Beside the bed was a wooden folding table that had served as kitchen table and desk, washstand and work-bench. A vegetable crate nailed to the wall acted as shelf and medicine cabinet. A sack of hand tools spilled onto the floor, their wooden handles long ago chewed away by salt-starved porcupines. A rusting hoard of Beehive corn syrup tins spoke of a man with a monumental sweet tooth. Perhaps the most curious thing about the cabin was the dozens of drawings that decorated the log walls. Sketches in faded pencil, smudged charcoal and India ink turned sepia with age were beautifully rendered on scraps of writing paper, brown grocery sacks and pieces of cardboard. A closer look revealed that the model was always the same; a singular woman, her large dark eyes stared out from each picture. An oval face, high cheekbones and a mouth set in a sensuous pout were framed by thick black hair, pulled back in a bun. A small mole to the right of her mouth left no doubt that the images were of the same beautiful woman, her face never aging, her youthful beauty captured forever upon the walls of this crude gallery.

"Who was he?" the boy asked.

"Just a man who wanted to be left alone."

"Who's she?" He pointed to the pictures.

"Don't know" his grandfather answered. "Must have been someone pretty special, though."

Don't know, his grandfather had said. But he knew this place
had a lot to do with the woman in the drawings.

They had been married in the fall of 1915 after summer courtship. Picnics and boat rides had soon led to love. Their parents
kept summer homes not far from one another and they had met at
the annual regatta.

He was a young art student who had put his education on
hold in order to fight for King and Country. She had been intent
on studying in Paris, but the war in Europe put her plans on hold.

Romance had blossomed quickly between them; long afternoons spent holding hands or drifting around the lake in a long
cedar strip canoe. Every day he would sketch her portrait, over and
over, studying her face, memorizing it; intense dark eyes, thick
black hair pulled back to reveal high cheekbones on an oval face.
Her soft full lips, pouting as though they had just been kissed,
filled him with an aching desire. The last touch on each sketch was
the small dark mole sitting like a punctuation mark to the right of
her mouth. He had proposed to her on the last day of the summer
season and they had been married one month later in the city. He
was tall and handsome in the khaki uniform of a lieutenant in the
King's army, she a vision in ivory satin. Two weeks later she was
waving him goodbye from the station platform.

Events moved quickly and he soon found himself immersed in a
world of mud, cold, filth and death. At night, he would lie huddled
in his little dugout and dream of her face, her soft skin, their last night
together, clinging to one another, not wanting to let go. He would
sketch her face from memory on the backs of her letters.

He had survived almost two years in the trenches when on
Easter Monday of 1917 at a place named Vimy Ridge an artillery
round of the creeping barrage fell short. Sizzling chunks of shrap-
nel tore into his back and shoulders, neck and head.

His wounds were so severe that the stretcher bearers passed

him over, carrying away others who they felt stood a better chance of survival. He spent all night lying on the battlefield, the cold seeping into the very marrow of his bones. She came to him just after midnight, begging him to be strong, reassuring him that everything would be alright.

The next morning, he was still alive when they came to collect the dead. At the aid station, they said he would take too much time, so they shot him full or morphine and sent him to a hospital farther behind the lines to die.

Yet still he clung to life. The doctors dug out most of the shell fragments. Some were left in his head and neck. They posed less danger where they were than would the surgery required to remove them.

As he awoke from the ether slumber, he again saw her face and he called her name.

From France, he was sent to a convalescent home in England. He struggled to regain his strength and mobility while several more operations relieved the constant headaches and somewhat lessened the severity of the seizures brought on by his wounds.

His days were filled with rehabilitation exercised, stretching and flexing savaged muscles, working for hours with Indian clubs to restore his strength. On warm and sunny afternoons, he would sit in the garden and sketch her face, dreaming of the life they would share, of children and home.

In the early spring of 1919, he received his orders to sail for home. He wrote her immediately with the good news.

Two days later, he got the telegram. She was gone, it said, influenza. Her fever had reached 105 degrees as her lungs filled with fluid. Her dark eyes had burned red, the sockets deep and rimmed with sickly blue circles. It had only taken four days.

He came home that summer to live the woods. He hunted and fished and traded odd jobs in lumber camps and mining operations for things nature didn't provide; tea and rice, boots and candles, ink and pencils. Beehive corn syrup. A window, a table, a bed. He never gave his name. He was known only as the Hermit.

On a winter's night in 1934, he had his last seizure. He thrashed about on the cabin floor for a long time before she came to him. Smiling, she told him that everything would be alright. Once again, they held each other. He died in her arms.

The scavengers of the forest scattered his bones.

The old man and the boy followed the downhill slope of the forest floor, heading around the back of the loop that would bring them out behind the cottage. They stopped once to watch a downy woodpecker stitch an old elm tree with holes, it's long beak machine-gunning into the bark searching for a late lunch. They tracked a deer for a little ways, following the deep imprints left in the soft earth by it's sharp, cloven hooves. All along the way, nuthatches ran crazily up and down the trunks of trees. Spruce trees oozed globules of golden pitch. Green shoots rose up through the pine straw, soon to bloom into jack-in-the-pulpits, fiddleheads and brilliant white trilliums.

Farther along, they came to a familiar landmark; an uprooted stump, a bullet riddled paint can lid nailed to the bark. Here the old man had taught the boy to shoot, first a pellet rifle and then, last fall, a .22. He had learned to hold the butt of the stock firmly into his shoulder, letting out his breath and sighting down the barrel with both eyes open, then slowly squeezing the trigger. *Don't pull the trigger,* his grandfather had said, *S-Q-U-E-E-Z-E it.*

The boy was a quick study with a fire arm, shooting left-handed, conscious of the bolt of the .22 recoiling towards his cheek. He would have been a good hunter, if only he could see any sense in killing for sport. Too many Disney films when he was young: Bambi's mother. Old Yeller.

They climbed out of the slight hollow and there was the cottage, just down the hill and across the road.

The old man had bought the lot the spring his grandson turned a year old, one hundred and sixty-two feet of shoreline and two hundred and thirty odd feet up to the road. He also owned the land on the other side of the road for two miles back into the forest, including the old log shack and most of the abandoned beaver pond.

He decided to build the cottage on the slope between the road and the lakefront. That whole summer was spent clearing the lot and staking out the building site. A small white and turquoise house trailer served as centre of operations. This was soon joined by the first permanent structure on the land, a one-hole outhouse of two-by-fours sheathed with chipboard.

Every weekend, chainsaws whined as spruce and cedar were felled and then sectioned and piled as future firewood. Only as many trees necessary to create a cottage site and a clear view of the lake were removed. A stand of birch hugging the shoreline to the east was left untouched. His wife had insisted.

Footings were poured in the fall. Work would begin the following spring as soon as the frost was out of the ground. That winter was spent planning and re-planning. Materials were ordered and delivery dates arranged. A water pump, a kitchen sink and a big brown oil stove were purchased and stored in a friend's garage.

By the next March, the plans were finalized and all the permits were in order.

Construction began in May. The old man, his son-in-law and an ever-changing crew of friends and relatives worked every weekend that spring, their sleeves pulled down and their heads shrouded in bug nets to ward off the biting black flies. The women acted as a clean-up crew, carrying away the end cuts of lumber and bits and pieces of plywood. They made the men sandwiches and poured them drinks. At night, they rubbed the soreness form their husband's shoulders and backs. The boy, just over two years old, ran around excitedly, exploring with delight this new and strange world, worrying his mother.

The cottage quickly began to take shape. To accommodate the slope, the front of the building was raised on four columns made up of twelve cinder blocks, stacked upon concrete piers. The rear of the structure was joined directly to the footings, at ground level. The floor joists were covered with plywood and the exterior walls were framed and raised. The men erected the inside support walls and partitions, then built the roof and ceiling joists in place. The roof was covered over in plywood, the exterior in black tin-test. The outside was finally finished with grey-white asphalt shingles and imitation-log siding, stained red-brown.

The floor plan of the cottage was simple and functional. Doors at either end opened into one large room that stretched across the entire front of the building, one end being the kitchen, the other serving as the living room. Picture windows set into the front wall allowed a magnificent view of the lake as well as the rocky far shore; grey and pink granite backed by thick stands of cedar, spruce, birch and even a few towering white pine. A wide doorway cut into the back wall of the living room opened to a narrow hallway which led to three bedrooms as well as the future bathroom. Here the old man hoped he would one day be able to sit, warm and dry while doing his business, free from the bother of mosquitoes feasting on his bare bottom.

Over the next two years, the interior would be completed. Mahogany plywood panelling covered the walls; linoleum and indoor/outdoor carpeting, the floors; acoustic ceiling tiles and electric light fixture covered the exposed roof joists and replaced the Coleman lanterns that had hung from them. Kitchen cabinets and a sheet-metal fireplace made the inside of the cottage organized and cozy.

Outside, a deck that stretched the full length of the cottage and wrapped around each side was soon added on, a perfect place to take the sun and enjoy the summer breezes. On warm, starlit nights, the old man and the boy would often unfold green canvas camp cots, unroll their sleeping bags and sleep outside, lulled by the soft sound of the forest.

A permanent dock provided mooring space for the fishing boat and a canoe. The attached boathouse was soon filled with the clutter of cottage activities; fishing poles, minnow traps and tackle boxes, life jackets, canoe paddles and boat oars, ropes and inner tubes, jerry cans and snowmobiles.

That fall, the crowning glory was added. A hole was dug behind the cottage and a holding tank was lowered into it and buried. The cottage now had a septic system. Sixty feet of weeping pipe drained away the grey water. As soon as it was ready to go, the first cold snap of winter hit, freezing the water supply pipe submerged in the lake. For the next six months the toilet was primed by hand, using a saucepan of water taken from a five gallon pail filled daily through a hole chopped through the lake ice. The outhouse was left in place, however, to serve as an emergency back-up. It was also used for matters of delicacy. A hand lettered pronouncement on the bathroom wall read *"If you think you'll stink, then take it outside!"*.

It was a good cottage.

The boy and the old man sat at the kitchen table, between them sat a cribbage board, a deck of cards and a plate that now held only crumbs of his grandmother's homemade fudge. For the past two hours, they had eaten the whole batch, while the old man patiently taught the boy to play crib. He himself had learned to play while in the army and he had been addicted to the game ever since. In teaching the boy, he hoped to create another opponent. The game had not proven social enough for his wife and his daughter and son-in-law much preferred euchre, saying crib depended too much on luck.

They played slowly, counting out each hand card-by-card, the old man pointing out missed points and letting the boy take them. When the youngster got better, they would play "muggins", each keeping for themselves any points overlooked by the other.

The boy showed his hand, a pair of eights and a pair of twos. A seven had been turned up in the cut. He studied the cards and began to count "Fifteen two . . . Fifteen four . . . and uh . . . two pairs is . . . eight . . . and . . . that's it."

"Good" the old man said. He held a pair of sixes, an eight and a nine. The seven gave him a good run also. "Fifteen two, fifteen four, fifteen six, two runs of three is another six, that's twelve and a pair makes it fourteen." He pegged off fourteen points on the board and reached for the crib hand.

He had discarded a queen and an ace while the boy had thrown a three and a jack. "Nothin' . . . damn."

The boy gathered the cards and began to shuffle awkwardly, stopping every couple of seconds to tuck wayward cards back into the deck.

"Papa?"

"Mmm?"

"That hermit guy," the mystery stranger had preyed on his mind all afternoon and evening. "what do you supposed made him live like that?"

"I don't know. Maybe he saw how cruel civilization could be. Maybe something bad happened to him. Maybe he just wanted to run away for a while and it got to be a habit. I guess he just wanted to be alone."

"He sure picked a good place." said the boy in a matter-of-fact voice.

The old man looked out across the lake. The sun had set, leaving a salmon glow over the west shore, wisps of cloud shadowed purple. The sky overhead was turning a deep, dark blue, Venus already brightly visible. The reflection of the sunset backlit the ripples on the surface of the lake, black strands dancing across the pink-tinged water, the silhouette of the trees dark against the sky.

The old man thought then about the hermit. He could somewhat understand the desire to run away. He'd known it himself at times, that urge to hop a freight train and lose yourself, away from jobs, mortgages, bills, responsibilities, free to ride the range with no concerns but the cattle and the drinks and the women waiting at the end of the trail. But then his wife would smile at him, his daughter would give him an unsolicited hug and all would again be right with the world. What could have happened to make a man decide to spend his life so alone? He could only imagine the torment, the sadness, the hopelessness, helplessness the other man must have felt. But, still, there must have been evenings like this one when the man would come to the edge of the lake to watch in peace and quiet as the sun went down. The boy's right, the old man thought, the man sure picked a good place.

The boy had dealt the cards and had already fed two into his crib. The old man gathered his cards in and looked at them: an ace, a two, a deuce, an eight, a jack and a king. Nothing.

"Who the hell dealt this mess." he said with disgust.

The boy let loose a devilish giggle. He loved to win.

CHAPTER 4

The traffic along highway 401 was not very heavy at quarter to twelve at night. The young man was making good time as the car drew closer to the airport. His mother was quiet in the seat beside him.

He had volunteered to pick his grandmother up at the terminal, knowing how his father hated big city driving, the multiple lanes and confusing web of on and off ramps raising his stress level to an unhealthy high.

As he approached the exit, he signalled and moved across two lanes, smoothly leaving the highway. Ahead lay the airport, passenger jets of all sizes and colours swarming around the twin terminals, loading and unloading their cargoes of passengers.

The car now entered the maze of ramps and roads that led to the multi-level parking garage. He pulled into a parking space just as the green digits on the dashboard clock flashed midnight. They hurried into the building, his grandmother's plane due in fifteen minutes.

They entered the concourse and checked the arrivals board. Her plane would be disembarking at gate five. It would also be one hour late.

He escorted his mother over to a row of orange plastic chairs and sat her down. At a nearby kiosk, he bought two cups of tea. Carrying them back to the lounge, he handed one of the Styrofoam cups to his mom, then sat down beside her. For a while, they sipped their tea in silence.

Then she started to talk.

Not about her father at first, only about the neighbourhood where she had grown up in his house, the house he'd built with his own hands. How at first, they had to use an outhouse and bathe in a galvanized washtub in the kitchen. How when they were finally connected to the town sewer and water systems, she stood flushing the toilet over and over again, amazed at what they would think of next.

She told of family trips, camping up north in a leaky canvas tent, the big trip to Florida in 1954, staying in a motel for the first time in her life, about the time the wheel fell of their '47 Buick on the way to her grandfather's house.

Gradually, the stories came to be about him. Her Father. Her Dad.

She didn't recognize him when he returned home in 1946. She was six years old and he had been overseas for three years, in the service for four. She cried his first night home because he was a stranger in her mother's house. She couldn't comprehend that this was the same man she had been sending messages to on the bottom of her mother's letters, scribbles giving way to first letters, then proudly and painstakingly printing her whole name, soon after adding "Luv". Finally, full letters of her own; "Dear Daddy. It is snowing. I went to visit gramma. I had cookies. I love you. Come home soon."

He worked hard to get settled after so much time away, working the midnight shift at the car plant, getting off the job at seven in the morning. He would make it home in time to have breakfast with her before seeing her off to school with a hug and a kiss on the cheek.

After he got onto steady-days, he helped coach her softball team and chaperoned the teen dances at the park clubhouse. She would always request Nat King Cole and take a turn with her dad around the dance floor.

Mother and son had shared these stories a hundred times. Yet, they still nodded their heads at the truth of a reaction or shook them at the absurdity of the situation. And they laughed. For the first time since they got the news of the old man's death, they laughed.

The passenger gates opened and people started filing through, mostly weary, happy tourists back from a week in the Florida sunshine. Families of sunburned parents towed tired offspring with pink ears and peeling noses, the smallest stragglers's asleep and drooling on dad's shoulder at this late hour.

Then he saw his grandmother standing at the gate, a travel bag clutched in both hands. He went to her and led her to where his mother sat. The two women hugged one another for a long time.

At the luggage carousel and retrieved her suitcases and he carried them to the car.

He sat alone in the front seat on the way home, his mother and grandmother in the backseat, talking about nothing in particular, anything to keep from thinking of the old man.

His grandmother would spend the night in the spare room of her daughter and son-in-law's house. Although it being late, she couldn't bring herself to turn out the light and go to bed alone. Instead, she began to unpack, putting her belongings away in the dresser drawers and closet. She opened the second case and lifted out her husband's navy-blue Legion blazer and hung it up, gently brushing the gold-crowned crest with the red maple leaf. She began to cry. She hung up his crisp white shirt and his grey flannel pants, hanging the powder blue striped tie over them. She returned to the case and looked inside. She began to laugh. She laughed until she had to sit down on the bed.

She had packed him extra socks and underwear.

"I don't imagine he'll be needing them," she said to herself.

She lay her head down and sighed, "Silly old fool." Then she fell asleep.

* * *

The July morning was only an hour old. Heavy dew turned the long grass silver. The small stream wandered gently through the abandoned farm field and a cedar split rail fence zig—zagged back and forth along its east bank.

For seven years shortly after the war, two brothers and their families had tried raising beef on pasture land carved into the north woods. It had been a hard go, but little-by-little they were making a life for themselves. Wolves would take a few calves each year, and the cattle had to be trucked a long way to the railhead, but the families' needs were few and they liked their lives.

Then, in the winter of '53, the eldest brother's house caught fire and he and his family lost everything. They moved in with the younger brother's family: four adults and seven children in a two-bedroom farmhouse only nine hundred feet square and a one hole privy out back.

A late, harsh spring left the herd weak and sickly, the mortality rate of the new born calves at almost forty percent. Then finally, the warmth returned to the sun, a new green grass shot up. The remaining calves stilted and frolicked in the pasture, the adults begin to put on fat. Things were finally looking up when the brucellosis hit. Within two weeks, the brothers watched their cattle cough their lives away. By the time they shot the last two cows, they had decided they would no longer be farmers.

The eldest moved back to the big city and got a job in a hardware store. Eventually, he would come to own it.

The younger brother moved his family north into asbestos country. After twenty-six years below ground, he retired on a disability. Five years later he, like his cattle, coughed himself to death.

In time, the land returned to the wild, native grasses and plants taking over the pastures. A wind storm several years ago reduced the remaining farmhouse to a pile of firewood. The fence rails along the road had been taken by cottagers and now lent their rustic charm to a hundred suburban ranch dwellings. Where cattle once grazed, foxes again hunted pheasants and field mice while high above, hawks rode the summer thermals, their eyes searching below for any movement that might mean a meal. The creek that watered the herd was now given over to scores of leopard frogs. Fishin' frogs.

Three creeping bodies cut three dark swaths through the wet grass. The old man and the boy were on the prowl for frogs. Joining them in the hunt was a third party.

Ed Miller had bought the cottage next door to the old man's a couple of years ago and had become a fairly constant companion of the old man, to the slight jealousy of the boy, and the great relief of Ed's wife, Marion. At first, the boy had tolerated his company only because Ed was constantly telling tall tales, spiced with sayings the boy had never heard before and with a string of the most imaginative obscenities that impressed even the old man. If he was to admit it, the boy had grown quite fond of old Ed.

"C'mon out ya goddamn slimy bastards", Ed was now calling. "I know yer hidin' in those weeds somewheres, ya' spotty little buggers."

The old man and the boy grinned at each other, amused at Ed's entreaties.

Ed's job was to walk along the very edge of the water, startling the frogs while simultaneously cutting off their escape route to the creek. The boy and the old man then took advantage of the frog's confusion and into the bucket it would go. After a hundred and fifty feet of hunting, the men were soaked to the knees with dew and richer by eleven frogs.

The three great white frog hunters carried the specialized weapons of their job. A loop of coat hanger wire was securely taped to a three foot length of broomstick. A woman's nylon stocking was then stretched over the wire, forming a sheer trap that would pin a frog to the ground. The frog would then be grasped through the stocking, picked up and popped into the bucket.

It was hard work, catching these little frogs. Long, thin and bony, emerald green backs covered with gold-edged black spots, the leopard frogs were lightning quick. Putting one in front of a smallmouth bass was like putting a sirloin steak in front of a starving tiger. To describe the fight the fish would put up, one only had to imagine trying to get the steak back.

"Yaaagh!" The calm morning air was suddenly rent by a hoarse cry.

Ed jumped two feet straight up in the air. When he landed, he began beating the ground with the handle of his frog trapper.

"Ya' scaly bellied sonofabitch!" Whack, whack. "Ya' goddamn creepy crawly bugger!" Whack, whack, whack.

The old man and the boy ran over to see what was the matter. An eighteen-inch garter snake was squirming through the grass, desperately trying to evade this crazed human who had disturbed its morning nap.

Finally, the stick broke and the snake made his escape. Ed was panting now, red-faced, sweat beading on his brow and upper lip. His thin white hair stuck up every which way.

"Goddamn sonofabitchin' striped-backed bastard!" Ed yelled after the fleeing reptile. Although he had spent his whole life in the woods, Ed had never gotten over his fear of snakes.

The boy and his grandfather sat on the ground, helplessly shaking with laughter. The old man took a coughing spell but continued to laugh, wiping his eyes with the back of his hand. The pail had overturned, the frogs jumping for the creek, desperate to reach the safety of the water.

"Goddamn it, what're ya's laughin' at? Ya never see a man fight off a snake before. An' besides that, look whatcha' done. The goddamn frogs is gettin' away." Ed gripped his broken net and started back toward the car. "To hell with ya's. Ta' hell with the goddamn frogs, too. Geezus H. Murphy! Me tryin' to fight off a snake and you two dumb bastards gigglin' away in the grass, lettin' all the goddamn frogs get away! Well, all I can say is 'ta hell with ya'. I don't need any goddamn frogs. I'll fish with a goddamn bare hook. An' quit'cher laughin'. See how funny ya think it is when one of them slitherin' bastards crawls up your leg."

It was five minutes before the old man and the boy were able to get up and follow him.

Ed had been raised in the bush country of Eastern Ontario. His father worked as a trapper and a guide and from the age of eight, Ed had joined his father in his work. Together, they worked a trapline over thirty five miles, taking the pelts of mink, beaver and muskrat, raccoon and wolf. Every so often, a trap might even hold a lynx or a bobcat, its hide worth a month's wages.

In the summer, they would guide American fisherman, showing them the best spots for muskie, bass and pickerel, a fish the Americans insisted on calling walleye. His father would supplement his fees by selling these wealthy sportsmen bottles of his special, secret "fish scent". By the age of twelve, Ed was helping his father manufacture the product, diligently chewing tobacco and spitting the juice into empty mickey bottles to be mixed with lake water and sold for five dollars each.

"Goddamn dumb Yankees", his father would say as they blended the concoction. "More money'n brains."

By the age of fifteen he was actively contributing to the supply of empty bottles.

It was about this time that Ed's mother decided she'd had enough of spruce trees, rocks and mosquitoes. One fall, Ed and his father contracted to guide a group of Ohio moose hunters. When the float plane lifted off the lake, one of them, a dentist from Akron, left with a bull moose, a bad cold and Mrs. Miller. Ed's father immediately got drunk and stayed that way.

The following spring, Mr. Miller took another bottle of Seagram's best and set out on the lake in his canoe. He was down to the last few swallows when a droning sound caught his attention. Overhead, he spotted a bright yellow Fairchild 71 float plane. It waggled its wings in warning, letting Ed's father know of its intention to land where the canoe was. It continued down the lake, banked out of sight behind the point and began its approach. It came in, lower and lower, touching down, throwing twin wakes up from its pontoons. The plane was now taxiing across the water, heading for the point and the mooring dock on the other side.

To his father's liquor-soaked brain, the plane suddenly meant only one thing: his whore of a wife and that sissy sonofabitch of an Akron dentist were coming back for the boy. Tears of loss and rage filled his eyes. No goddamn way were they taking the boy. He picked up a paddle and steered the canoe for the point.

Ed had been stretching a fox pelt outside the cabin door when he heard the airplane. Even though float planes came and went a dozen times a year on the lake, Ed never tired of watching them land. He always hurried to the mooring dock to tie the aircraft up and to help unload passengers (customers?) and their gear; expensive rods and reels, hunting rifles and shotguns with walnut stocks and intricately engraved mechanisms. Today was no different. He finished the knot he was tying and propped the stretching frame against the cabin wall. He brushed off the seat of his trousers and headed for the dock. He got there in time to see his father in his canoe heading for the point. The engine of the Fairchild thrummed louder, now.

"What the hell . . . ?", Ed thought out loud.

His father rose unsteadily in the canoe and brandished his paddle like a battle axe.

"C'mon ya' lousy bastards! Yer not takin' my boy away! Ya' hear me? Yer not gettin' him!".

He was sobbing now and took several awkward swipes at the air with his paddle.

The pilot taxied around the point, keeping a close eye on the shore side for shallow rocks and deadheads. Behind him, a party of Detroit auto executives jabbered excitedly about the fish they hoped to soon catch. The pilot turned his attention to the front of the aircraft in time to see a wavering figure standing in green canvas canoe directly ahead. The man swung the paddle, his face twisted in a scream of hate and desperation.

Ed's father had cleared the point at the same time as the airplane. He fixed his defiance on the blur of the spinning propeller. He swung the paddle.

"He's all I've got left!", he cried.

The follow through of the swing threw him off balance and he fell headfirst into the wooden blades of the prop. The pilot killed the power at the last second but it was too late. Splinters of bone and shreds of tissue, red and grey, spattered the nose of the plane.

Ed watched in mute horror as his father's headless body pitched forward into the bottom of the canoe that now rode between the airplane's yellow-painted floats.

"Poor old bugger . . . ," he said finally, his voice flat.

An hour later on the dock, one of the auto executives pulled the pilot aside. He reached into the pocket of his custom-tailored bush pants and pulled out a wad of bills. He peeled off a twenty and tucked it into the breast pocket of the pilot's jacket.

"How long do you think it'll take us to get another guide in here?", he asked.

Two months later, Ed packed his few belongings and moved into the city.

The boat drifted over the weed-bed, pushed along by a light breeze that blew straight down the lake. The old man sat in the stern, the boy in the bow, both easily casting into pockets in search of smallies. Three already swam clipped to the chain stringer the dangled over the side of the boat.

Ed sat in the middle seat, his rod held between his knees. He was hunched over secretively, tying on a new lure. His parsnip nose was mere inches away from his hands, his wiry white eyebrows knitted together in myopic concentration as he squinted at his handiwork.

"Whatsa' matter, Ed, forget your glasses?", the old man grinned. He loved to tease Ed. Usually it elicited an amusing and profane response.

"No I didn't forget my goddamn glasses, smart ass. Anyhow, I don't need cheaters to tie on no sonofabitchin' lure. I can do that in my goddamn sleep."

The boy picked up on his grandfather's lead.

"What'cha all hunched over for then, Ed?", he asked innocently.

Ed finished the knot and clipped the end of the line with his teeth. Hiding the lure in the palm of his hand, he raised his head to address his tormentors.

"Geezus H. Murphy, I'm only tryin' to be sportin'. This here lure I'm holdin' is so potent and powerful, well, if the fish saw me tyin' it on, they'd be jumpin' right into the goddamn boat. You two sorry buggers wouldn't stand a chance. Why, every fish in the goddamn lake'd be floppin' around in the bottom of the boat an' there wouldn't be so much as a dinky old sunfish left for you two sonofabitchin' hyenas".

Indeed, the old man and the boy were laughing out loud by this time. Ed shook his shaggy head and picked up his rod. Bringing the lure to his mouth, he spat on it for luck and cast it out. He had a fish on before he was halfway through his retrieve.

"Here it is, here it is! C'mere you little beauty. Goddamn it, I told you sonsabitches this lure was powerful!".

The old man and the boy looked at one another and, grinning increduously, could only shake their heads.

Ed's sayings, "Edisms" the boy came to call them, never failed to both produce a smile and accurately describe the given situation.

A fish that completely swallowed a baited hook was a "hungry-gutted sonofabitch."

A homely woman was "uglier'n a barrel full of crushed arseholes."

A slow-witted or stupid person was "dumber than a bag of hammers" and conversing with them was like "talkin' to a goddamn stump."

To flatten out a parking spot behind his cottage, Ed called in a man with a "bullnoser".

Any man guided by lust was "lettin' the little head do the thinkin' for the big one."

He once announced to a boatful of fishermen that he was in a foul mood because he "woke up with a perfectly good hard-on for the first time in five years" and then "just pissed it away".

He referred to his wife's beloved cat, Muffin, as "that furry goddamned speed bump."

The lake had been busy for two weeks. Summer holidays had brought to the lake friends and relatives, all of whom contributed to the "Annual End of Summer Holidays Fish Fry and Corn Roast."

They gathered at dusk around the outdoor stone fireplace that stood beside Ed and Marion's cottage. A hardwood fire had been burning since mid-afternoon and in the two iron skillets on top, the bacon grease was two inches deep and spitting, full of fish fillets turning golden in the aromatic bath. A bushel basket of corn had been shucked and the boy's mother was now dropping the creamy yellow cobs into a huge pot. On a nearby picnic table, bowls of cole slaw sat, light green, white and creamy. Potato salad, sliced eggs and paprika decorating the top, sweated in a big steel mixing bowl. Plates of sliced, homegrown tomatoes and cucumbers in a vinegar and mayonnaise sauce fought for space with baskets of buns and loaves of bread. The nearby fish-cleaning table had been pressed into service as a bar. Bottles of rye and rum and a bucket of ice waited to sacrifice themselves in the name of insobriety. On the ground beside the table in a galvanized washtub of ice water, stubby brown bottles of beer and cans of pop floated.

A breeze blew in lightly off the lake and combined with the cool of the late July evening to keep the mosquitoes at bay. The smell of woodsmoke mixed with the aroma of frying fish set mouths to watering and sharpened appetites.

The timing was perfect. The first batch of fish was finished at exactly the same time as the first potful of corn.

"Come and get it while it's hot."

The old man lifted out pieces of tender, crumb-covered bass and placed them in a bowl lined with paper towel. The skillets were quickly refilled for seconds and thirds.

Corn was placed on platters and carried to the table.

Paper plates were soon piled high. Pieces of fish disappeared into mouths, followed by rapid inhalations and fanning hands as hot grease scalded tender tongues. Teary eyes followed by a swig of cold beer elicited a "Damn, that's good fish!" In went another piece.

Cobs of succulent new corn were rolled over and over in dollops of butter, then salted. Some ate their corn in neat rows, others ate around the cob. Some simply took random bites, turning the cob over and over hunting for a likely spot, then darting in, pecking away a mouthful of kernels. Melted butter dripped from wrists and elbows and ran down chins where it was sucked from fingers and licked off the sides of hands.

The eating went on until the fish was finally gone, only greasy paper towel and bread crumbs left in the bowl. Corn cobs stripped clean of their kernels sat in congealing puddles of butter and salt. The bowls of salad were all but empty, leaving only creamy spoon scrapes around the sides. One forlorn slice of tomato remained on the plate, drowning in its own juice.

Around the clearing, people sat on lawn chairs, bellies full and lips filmed with grease. They grinned guiltily at each other, the battle against the sin of gluttony lost.

Slowly, energy began returning. Conversations began. Jokes were told and the laughter grew. The kids began moving around again.

Ed appeared with a battered fiddle. He tightened and rosined the bow and brought the strings into approximate tune. Tucking the instrument under his chin, he warmed up with a couple of short licks, then launched into "St. Anne's Reel." Jigs and logger's tunes followed in quick succession, people clapping their hands and stomping their feet. When Ed began "The Log Driver's Waltz," several couples got up and danced, the boy was amused to see his parents among them. His father usually considered these evenings hokey. Yet there they were, gliding in effortless unison beneath the trees, his father's lead gracefully strong and sure. What surprised the boy most though, was the expression on their faces. He was too young to know its full meaning, but he knew that, tonight, while they danced, the rest of the world ceased to exist.

They were no longer merely parents, but two people completely safe and comfortable in each other's arms and the boy came to the awkward realization that his parents were a man and a woman very much in love.

The song ended and the spell was broken. The dancers returned to their seats, some laughing and talking, others, like his parents, embarrassed by their public display of affections walked back stiff and formal, his father holding his mother's elbow.

Another old fellow from a few cottages down had retrieved an old flat top guitar, a pre-war Gibson, it's sunburst top dark and checkered with age and use. He sat down on the picnic table bench and proceeded to pick and sing his way through a blistering rendition of "Rocky Top" followed by bluegrass classics "Salty Dog," "Blue Moon of Kentucky" and "Rollin' In My Sweet Baby's Arms." A dip into the Hank Williams songbook produced "Hey Good Lookin'," "Your Cheatin' Heart" and a deliciously nasal "I'm So Lonesome I Could Cry" had several of the dancers up again and scuffling dirt, although the boy's parents sat this one out.

The old man was enjoying this night and his pleasure increased tenfold as Hank Williams segued into Hank Snow's "I've Been Everywhere," and Wilf Carter's "Strawberry Roan." Finally! Cowboy music!

The descending, Spanish-flavoured intro of "El Paso" and the old man tipped his head back and closed his eyes, a smile on his lips. He looked over to where the boy sat on the ground, one foot tucked beneath him, one knee up, distractedly tracing designs in the dirt with a stick. *Wonder what's wrong with him?* thought the old man. *He usually likes this music. Oh, well, maybe he ate too much or something.*

The picker finished the song and said he had to treat a case of sore fingers by wrapping them around a cold glass of rye. One of his young sons slipped into his place. About twenty four, he had dark shoulder length hair. *Looks like a goddamn girl,* the old man thought. He wore a denim jacket, faded and frayed and, around his neck on a macrame strap, hung a Martin D-28, it's book-matched spruce top glowing amber in the firelight. A percussively strummed blues progression intro'ed the first tune.

> *"Well I met a gin soaked bar room queen in Memphis,*
> *She tried to take me upstairs for a ride."*

The younger people began nodding and tapping, bobbing and weaving. The older faces became masks of polite tolerance. The old man detested this kind of music, as well as the lifestyle that went with it. The truth was, he found the unfamiliarity of it a little bit frightening. Men with long hair and beads. Crazy clothes. Crazy dances. Songs with lewd, screaming, often cryptic and indecipherable lyrics. Pounding drums, thumping basses and screeching guitars replaced beautiful melody with hammering, wailing rhythm. He looked again at the boy.

With the first chords, they boy's head had shot up. He now sat with his knees raised, both feet in front of him keeping time, one on an imaginary bass pedal, the other working a make-believe hi-hat cymbal. His left hand tapped out the bass beat on his knee while the right copied the guitarist's strum pattern against his thigh. He had recently become a follower of this new sound, ever since he'd stumbled across a station on his little red leather transistor radio that was playing Top-Forty rock. He abandoned his search for a country-western station and sat enthralled, as that afternoon he discovered not only a new style of music but a new culture as well. Instead of songs about gunfighters and cattle drives, he heard a man declare himself to be a walrus. Goo Goo Ga Joo. He had no idea what it meant, but he loved it. Instead of riding tall in the saddle off into the sunset, he now longed to get his "motor runnin'" and "head out on the highway." Of course, he had heard the music before, but only peripherally. Now, suddenly, he'd found a soundtrack for whom he was becoming, for who he wanted to be. These musicians and the characters they sang of were *his* rebels, *his* outlaws and the world they moved in was *his* frontier. At the age of thirteen, he had found *his* cowboys.

His grandfather watched him, gyrating, tapping, drumming, an intense smile on his face. The hair that reached almost to the boy's collar and brushed the tops of his ears was not "summer shag" as the old man had thought, but the beginnings of *long* hair. He sang along to these strange lyrics, stories about "alligator lizards in the air", and tales of someplace called "Alice's Restaurant". It sounded like nonsense to the old man, but each song was rewarded with the boy's applause.

The old man shook his head slowly, sadly. The boy, once so much an extension of himself, was growing into a stranger.

He felt sad and something else. What? Like a good friend was moving away. They would always be friends, of course, but not in the same old way, the familiar old way. They would have to adjust to one another and adapt to the changes brought about by distance, in this case not of miles, but of generations. He guessed he always knew it would happen, he just didn't think it would happen so soon.

"I wonder when he stopped wanting to be a cowboy?", he whispered to himself.

The next day brought bad weather. Most everyone had left for home by noon. The old man and his wife were staying an extra week and the boy was staying with them.

A light curtain of rain had fallen all through the morning, turning heavy just after lunch. Outside the living room window, the trees dripped darkly while a northerly wind chopped the surface of the lake, whitecaps forming on the crests of the waves. Inside, a small fire burned in the fireplace, warding off the dampness.

The boy lay on the floor, a stack of comic books scattered around him. His favourites had always been the westerns: Kid Colt, Two-Gun Kid, Rawhide Kid, Geronimo Jones. However, these dog-eared issues, read and re-read hundreds of times, were at this moment being ignored. Instead, the boy was immediately engrossed in the latest issue of "Mad" magazine. Satirical and irreverent, it entertained the boy, confused his grandfather and for some reason, frightened his mother. This immediately raised the esteem of the magazine in the boy's eyes.

The old man sat on one end of the couch, a pad of paper on his thigh. He held his head high in the air and peered down over his nose at the pencil marks he had made, trying to bring the figures into focus. *I'm either going to have to get reading glasses, or longer arms,* he thought to himself. He took the pencil from it's resting place behind his ear and scratched a few more figures on the paper.

On the other end of the couch, his grandmother read her check-out line tabloid, disgusted at the thought of what that nice television father was doing with three, three mind you, naked prostitutes in his swimming pool. It had to be true or they couldn't print it, could they?

His grandfather made a final note on the pad, then paused, tapping the eraser end of the pencil against his teeth.

"Well, if we're gonna retire here, I figure we're gonna need to put in a basement." He nudged the boy with his toe. "You game to help?"

"Shouldn't we wait for it to stop raining first?" the boy grinned.

"I was thinkin' more of next summer, smart ass."

"Oh, well then. How are we gonna do it?" The boy sat down on the couch beside his grandfather and took up the pad.

"Hafta dig her out by hand. Not enough room to get equipment under there. Pour a cement pad. Probably hafta do that by hand too. I don't think a mixer could get in here. Cement block walls. That should do it."

"Lotta work. Whaddya' gonna use it for?"

"Furnace, hot water heater. Soon's I do that, we can put in a bathtub and a shower."

"Shower'd be nice if we're gonna be doing all that work", the boy observed.

"Well" said the old man, "I'm also gonna need a work shop.

Maybe store the snow machines down there too. Might even get a ping pong table." The old man was nuts about ping pong.

"Sounds good" said the boy.

"Well, let's plan it later. Right now, I feel like kickin' somebody's butt at crib." He looked at the boy.

"You can try."

"Go get the cards."

On the other end of the couch, his grandmother smiled. *They sure do get along,* she thought. *Well, no wonder, they're so much alike.*

She returned her attention to her reading, drawn to the headline "Cow Gives Birth to Human Baby." She shook her head "Now even I don't believe that one," she smiled.

CHAPTER 5

His parents were taking his grandmother to select a casket and to make the funeral arrangements. Plans were also made to have the body passed through customs and delivered to the funeral home for preparation. The young man's father took charge, protecting his mother-in-law from the avarice of the sales-pitch intended to prey upon the fragile emotions of the recently widowed. They then contacted the local newspaper and placed the death notice and obituary.

Meanwhile, the young man had volunteered to drive his sister to university, one hundred and fifty miles away. She was scheduled to begin her exams that week and she needed to make arrangements that would allow her to attend the funeral. With her high marks, it should not be a problem, only a formality.

The morning broke cold and clear and they were on the road by half-past seven, driving into the rising sun.

They drove in silence for a while, then slowly began making small talk. It wasn't until almost an hour had passed that talk turned to their grandfather.

His sister started. "This reminds be of the morning Nana and Papa and I left for Florida." Six years earlier they had taken her to Disney World over Christmas (the young man's trip with them had been to the west coast when he was ten). She talked of how they rode Space Mountain and Pirates of the Caribbean, Captain Nemo's Submarine and the Jungle Cruise. She told of spending New Year's Eve in a motel room with another family they had met down there, everyone dressed in bed sheet togas and hotel shower caps, watching Dick Clark on TV and singing "Auld Lang Syne" at midnight.

He in turn shared stories of travelling across northern Ontario, standing with his grandfather on an outcrop over the French River, drinking out of a rocky basin on the north shore of Superior and running out of gas just west of Thunder Bay. He told about how their grandmother would get exasperated by her husband's habit of stopping at every historical marker and pioneer cemetery along the way.

They both laughed as he recalled using a pay shower at a campground just outside Edmonton. The old man knew the shower was on a timer, but he forgot to warn the boy. After luxuriating under his first hot shower in almost a week, the youngster had just finished soaping himself when the water shut off. Hearing his name called, the old man opened the shower door to find the boy standing forlornly, covered head to toe in rapidly drying soapsuds.

"I ran out of water" the boy said.

The old man had only brought enough change for two showers, one each. He would have to walk back to the trailer for more coins. He put on his pants and pulled a sweatshirt over his head. Slipping on his shoes, he told the boy he would be right back.

"Please hurry," the boy begged, "I'm really starting to itch."

"Okay! Okay! I'll be back in a couple'a minutes." He couldn't resist a parting shot. "Don't get yourself in a lather." He chuckled to himself all the way back to the campsite.

They kept up a running conversation for the rest of the trip, laughing through the halls of the limestone university buildings, remembering inside jokes and stories dredged up form their childhoods.

It wasn't untilover lunch that they really began to catch up, talking in a way they hadn't for a long time. She had only just started high school when he began college. Schoolwork, part-time jobs and boyfriends and girlfriends took up most of their time. She enrolled in university the same year he was married. While he and his wife were building a new life for themselves, she was a freshman over one hundred and fifty miles away. He realized his sister was now a young woman, not the fourteen-year-old girl he remembered her to be. He found out she was in love, that they were even discussing marriage.

"We'd like to wait at least a year after graduation. He may have to travel to find a job."

"Is that okay with you?"

"Yeah, I think so. I'll be able to find a job almost anywhere. I know it'll be hard on mom and dad, but life's full of hard choices isn't it?" She almost had herself convinced.

He wouldn't have had the guts to even consider moving away from the security of his hometown. He had planned his future around what was offered at the local community college and had then settled for a safe job close to home. He greatly admired the courage and independence of his sister, her ability to know what she wanted and the guts to go after it.

Her fiance-to-be had already been in touch with several corporations, any one of which could take him not only anywhere across North America, but anywhere around the world. The idea did scare her a little, but she also found the idea exciting and liberating. She would find the freedom to re-invent herself, to break away from her existing persona.

He knew, though, that no matter where she went, she would carry the imprint of their family. She was destined to be a supportive and loving wife, a devoted and gentle mother, a conscientious and dedicated worked and a fiercely loyal and dependable friend.

On the way home that afternoon, the late winter sun shone through the car windows, warming the interior. The boredom of being a passenger, combined with seemingly endless landscape of winter-weary farmland, dull browns, contrasting with featureless white, made her drowsy. The motion of the car, gently bumping along the highway. The tires singing their monotonous lullaby put her to sleep.

As he drove, he knew that the last few hours had changed their relationship forever. They would never again be children, brother and sister, locked in sibling rivalry, teasing and pestering one another. They were now adults, best of friends, linked by common bonds of understanding forged by a shared upbringing, raised with the same ethics of responsibility and compassion, honesty and loyalty.

Never again would one wish the other would "get lost." Not just when they were finding each other again.

* * *

The old man and the boy leaned over opposite sides of the crumbling concrete of the small bridge, hauling up minnow traps hanging from lengths of clothesline rope. The mesh cylinders with concave open-ended cones at either end, had been baited with bread and suspended from the bridge supports the night before, dangling just below the surface of the sluggish little creek. The minnows, attracted by the bread, swam up the cones and through the small openings. Once inside, they lacked the memory or power of reason to find their way back out.

The traps were heavy with minnows. Quickly the man and boy undid the clasps that held the mesh halves together and dumped the squirming, shining catch into two minnow pails, at least a couple of dozen in each. One pail they would keep for themselves, one pail they were collecting for Ed, next door.

"Looks like we got some good ones" the old man said.

"Should catch a lot of bass with these, that's for sure."

"Well, let's get 'em home before they die on us."

They swished the traps through the water a few times to rinse away the remains of the soggy bread, then put the traps and the minnow pails in the trunk of the maroon Impala.

They climbed in the front seat and started down the road, grateful for the breeze blowing in through the open windows. Two-forty air-conditioning, the old man called it. Two windows down and forty miles an hour. It was only nine thirty in the morning, but the August day was already shaping up to be a scorcher.

The tires thumped over the ridges of the old corduroy road, gravel snapping from under the treads. A fine dust plumed in

their wake and settled in a film on the Queen Anne's lace, black-
eyed Susans, tiger lilies and daisies along the roadside.

"Gotta stop at the store and pick up some Coke for Uncle
Alex" the old man said.

"Uncle Alex" was the old man's big brother. He would drink
only Canadian Club rye mixed with Coca-Cola. Nothing else would
do. The old man couldn't understand how anyone could drink
such a disgusting concoction let alone waste good rye by mixing it
with syrupy sweet soda pop. But, it was what his brother drank, so
he would stop for the Coke. He had already poured the bargain-
basement rye into the Canadian Club bottle he kept beneath the
kitchen sink. He had been "upgrading" cheap rye for his brother
like this since he got smart twelve years ago. His brother never
knew the difference.

Six years separated the two brothers, Alex being the oldest,
and as brothers go, the two were as different as night and day.
Whereas the old man was short, bow-legged and casual about his
appearance, his older brother was over six feet tall, a dapper moustache adorning his upper lip. His hair was brushed back hard from
his forehead. Even in the relaxed surroundings of the cottage, he
wore neatly pressed slacks, Hunt Club polo shirts and cardigans
and tasselled loafers. He insisted on the best and wore designer
labels as badges of his minor executive success. When it came to
prestige, money was no object. For this, the old man constantly
teased him.

The two brothers began their lives on a tiny subsistence farm
along the north shore of Lake Ontario. Alex was born in 1914, the
old man following in 1920. A sister was born in 1922, only to die
in infancy during her first winter.

The family scraped a living out of their small patch of ground
until 1925 when a series of setbacks framed by a late spring and an
early killing frost, left them eating nothing but porridge for two
straight months. Just after the New Year, they moved to a boarding house in the nearby city, giving the farm to the county in lieu

of back taxes. Their father secured employment in the automobile factory, while their mother cleaned the houses of the town's wealthier citizens.

At twelve years of age, Alex was acutely aware of his poverty. Although his clothes were always freshly laundered and pressed, there was no disguising the fact that they were frayed at cuff and collar, mended and patched at elbow and knee. Often they were poorly fitting hand-me-downs from the families his mother worked for. His classmates would often amuse themselves by identifying articles of his clothing that had previously been theirs.

At six years of age, the old man was not so painfully aware of his family's poverty. Indeed, the move to the city introduced him to such luxuries as steam heat, meat *and* vegetables for each evening meal and, wonder of wonders, electricity. By the time he reached the age where social status was important, his family had moved into a house of their own and money was, if not rolling in, at least sufficient for them to be comfortable.

For Alex, however, the stigma of those early years of struggle would mark him for life. He would constantly battle to rise above his life as the son of a failed farmer turned factory worker and a common charwoman who spent her days on her knees scrubbing other people's dirt. At the age of seventeen, he could bear this shame no longer. He could feel nothing but contempt for his illiterate father who signed his first paycheck with an "X" and his only slightly more educated mother, she having completed fourth grade before leaving to help raise her six brothers and sisters.

After Alex finished high school, the father of a friend offered him a job as a clerk with a small manufacturing firm and he jumped at the opportunity. He would not spend his life sweating away on the factory floor or mopping other people's toilets. His first paycheck was spent on a double breasted navy pinstripe suit, the first new suit he had ever owned.

He was certainly not lazy and quickly advanced himself in the firm, working twelve hour days, six days a week. He learned to golf, joining the "in" country club. He also acquired in quick succession, a studio flat, a '32 Ford Roadster and a girlfriend. The daughter of a silk-stocking socialist, she found a certain self-righteousness in dating a boy who had grown up so poor. They were married three months before the outbreak of World War II.

Alex decided to do his patriotic duty and enlisted in early 1940. His new father-in-law called in a few political favours, and soon the young newlywed was a lieutenant in His Majesty's army. Daddy-in-law's influence ended there, however, and soon he found himself in Italy, cold and wet and muddy. He also found himself living, eating, sleeping, fighting and dying alongside dirt farmers and factory workers, men who had been raised by mothers who were cooks and charwomen, laundresses and sweatshop seamstresses. Their fathers had supported their families though the depression by stealing coal from railyards and doing any odd job that came along, putting their family's well-being ahead of their own personal pride. While Alex's father-in-law had sympathized with the plight of the working man as an abstract idea, these men had stared down the army, the police, the company's hired thugs and the government, demanding the right to be treated with the respect due any human being.

He soon came to respect these men, his admiration for their courage and loyalty superceding his previous contempt for their impoverished backgrounds and their lack of refinement. He also began to see the nobility of his parents, their hard work and their sacrifices, trying their best under very difficult circumstances to provide for him and his brother. His desire to make something of himself was no longer driven by a need to escape his upbringing, but to pay a debt of sorts to the efforts of his parents.

He came home in the fall of 1946 and resumed his career and his marriage. He also began mending fences. His father and mother welcomed him back with open arms. He was, after all, their oldest son and how well he was doing for himself. Anyone could see their pride when he and his pretty wife would pull up in their brand-new Buick. He lavished his parents with expensive gifts, gold cufflinks and silk ties, a Persian lamb's wool coat with a fox-fur collar.

The old man was not so quick to forgive. He could not forget how his brother had once turned his back on his family, on him. He well remembered the day he was walking his mother home from work and he spotted his brother coming the other way, a young lady on his arm. His brother saw them at the same moment and hurriedly steered the girl across the street to the opposite sidewalk. If his mother had noticed, she didn't let on.

He also remembered the day his brother pulled into the gas station where the old man worked after he had quit school at the age of fifteen. It was a hot August day, a furnace wind mixing with the gas fumes to create a foul miasma the sapped the old man's strength. His khaki shirt was dark with sweat, his peaked cap limp and sodden in the swelter. It was late afternoon when his brother pulled into the pumps, the convertible top of the coupe stowed in it's boot. Beside his brother sat a beautiful blonde who immediately began re-rouging her already perfect lips. Another couple sat in the back seat, the young man airily expounding the glories of fascism while at the same time trying to slip a less-idealistic hand under the young lady's skirt

Alex shut off the ignition and, looking his brother square in the chest, ordered a full tank.

"Check the oil while you're at it", he ordered. "Oh, and get the windshield, too.".

The old man stared at his brother who shot a furtive, guilty glance back at him. It was obvious the young playboy didn't want his new friends to know that this sweaty, little gas jockey was his brother.

"C'mon, let's step to it, boy. We haven't got all day.".

Beside him, the blonde tittered and playfully swatted his arm, admonishing him for his rudeness towards the hired help.

"Yes . . . sir". The old man spat out the words.

He hurriedly completed the tasks set out for him by his brother, then returned to the driver's side where he received payment and made change. His brother tilted his head, inspecting the now-spotless windshield. He started the engine, revving it loudly.

"Good job", he allowed. "Get yourself a Coke".

He flipped a nickel just out of the old man's reach. It landed on the oil soaked gravel at his feet.

"Nice catch," commented the blonde as the convertible pulled away.

He looked down at the nickel.

"Asshole," he muttered. Turning on his heel, he left the nickel in the dirt.

The turnaround didn't come until their father passed away in the summer of 1952. The old man made all the funeral arrangements himself, refusing his brother's repeated offers of help.

A few days after the funeral, he went to his parent's house to retrieve some insurance papers. He found his brother in front of the hall closet, kneeling, the contents of a cardboard box spread on the floor in front of him. A ruled exercise book lay open in his brother's lap. He was slowly running his hand over the pages. When he looked up, his eyes were red and swollen and tears ran unchecked down his cheeks. Wordlessly, he handed over the book.

Every line was the same. Their father's signature written over and over in a cramped, childlike scrawl, the result of hour upon hour of painstaking practice. Page by page the writing improved, growing more confident, losing its shakiness. Finally, the pencil gave way to ink.

"What . . . ?".

"You mean 'why', don't you? Every night for a couple of months. Mom taught him. He'd get out his jack knife and put a new point on his pencil. Then he'd write his name over and over. He'd be hunched over with his nose damn near on the paper. He did it because of you. Because he remembered how embarrassed you would get, watching him make his "X". Goddamn you!", he was yelling now. "Goddamn you to hell!"

His brother took the book back and again touched his father's name. A fresh tear plopped on the page, blurring a pencil line.

"I'm sorry. I'm sorry I treated them the way I did for so long. I'm sorry for everything. I know they did their best. I know. And

I'm sorry for the way I treated you. I wasn't any kind of big brother for you. I'm sorry for that." He looked up, his eyes wet, his nose streaming into his neatly trimmed moustache. "I'm sorry about the nickel." He dropped his head back down to the book.

The old man looked down at his brother. He knelt beside him, staring at the book.

"Goddamn you" he said again, though now without any conviction or malice.

He put his arm around his brother's shoulder and they sat for a long time.

The Impala pulled into the cottage store in a whirl of dust.

"You comin' in?"

The boy nodded and reached for the door handle.

"Good, you can help spend my change."

They both grinned and got out of the car.

The cottage store was a low, one-story building, sided with weathered white-painted clapboard. The black-shingled roof was encrusted with moss and lichen where a stand of spruce over hung one corner. Red plywood cut-out letters rising from the roof announced "GROCERIES" and a row of various sized deer antlers adorned the eaves.

The only other colour on the building came from a large orange and green tin 7-Up sign nailed to the wall.

A teenage boy in an oil stained "Keep On Truckin'" t-shirt came over wiping his hands on his grimy jeans. A broken-billed red cap advertising Champion Spark Plugs was pushed back from his forehead. When the Impala pulled in, he'd had his head buried beneath the cowling of a bright orange Moto-Ski snowmobile.

"Mornin'" he said to the old man.

"Mornin'. Sure is shapin' up to be a hot one."

"Yes sir, sure is."

"See what ya' squeze into her, willya'?"

"Yes sir." The teen moved to the bright yellow gas pump that sat on it's concrete island in front of the store. He lifted the nozzle and set the lever into the on position. Walking to the back of the car, he flipped down the licence plate, unscrewed the gas cap and inserted the nozzle. He began to fill the tank, the plastic balls bouncing in the glass bubble on the side of the pump.

"Check your oil?"

"Naw, it should be okay. If you could get the windshield, I'd appreciate it, though."

"Sure thing."

He locked the trigger and picking up a spray bottle and an old towel from the top of the pump, went to work on the dead bugs hardened on the windshield.

The old man and the boy entered the store through the wooden screen door decorated with the tin Pepsi-Cola push bar. There was a jingle of bells followed by a loud slap as he spring hinge closed the door against flies and wasps that lazily buzzed outside.

A woman about ten years older than the old man was busy sponging out the inside of the dairy cooler. The lady was quite petite with a home perm growing out of her salt and pepper hair. She wore pink pedal-pushers and a short-sleeved flowered blouse with white canvas deck shoes on her feet. A bucket of warm sudsy water sat on the floor beside her.

"Mornin' Marjorie. Keepin' cool?" the old man called out.

"A day like this, I can't think of a better place to be than the inside of a refrigerator."

"Ain't that the truth" the man agreed.

Marjorie was the owner of the store. Once married to a logger, she moved to the area with him, bringing along two small daughters. The following year, a kick-back tree limb made her a widow. She thought about returning to the city, but then realized she had come to love this northern country. With her husband's life insurance money and an iron determination, she bought the general store and set about raising the two girls alone. At first it wasn't easy, but they made the best of it, living in the storeroom out back. By day, she sold dry goods and gasoline to loggers and fishermen, as well as to the few cottagers who vacationed on the lake.

At night, in the back room, she would tutor the girls, teaching them from second-hand textbooks. When the Ministry of Education finally decided to investigate, they discovered the girls tested nearly two grades ahead of their age groups.

With the coming of the 'sixties, the cottage industry on the lake exploded. City folk, wealthy from post-war prosperity, sought solace amidst the northern forest, calming themselves to the sound of waves lapping the rocky shore.

As the cottage craze boomed, so did business. Every Friday night, carload after carload of families pulled into the store, stocking up for the weekend. The traffic continued all day Saturday. The same cars pulled in on Sunday night, gassing up for the trip back to the city.

The oldest girl married a local boy who worked as a jack-of-all-trades, building cottages and additions to cottages, docks and boathouses. He installed septic systems and drove the honey wagon that pumped them out. She continued to help her mother run the store. Her son was now pumping gas into the old man's car.

The youngest moved into the nearby town when she married the manager of the Brewer's Retail. She gained her real estate licence and made a killing selling vacation properties.

Later, as snowmobiling gained in popularity, Marjorie kept the store open all year round. Soon, she was doing almost as much business in the winter months as she did during the height of summer.

Eventually, she moved into a fine new home nestled amongst the cedars on a hill over-looking the store. Sometimes at night, she would lie in bed as the platinum moon washed her room in light. Outside her window, a breeze would whisper in the trees and an owl might announce the beginning of his night's work. Then she would think of her husband and her life. After a long while, she would close her eyes, smiling, and thank him for bringing her here.

The boy loved coming to the store. In the city, stores meant huge sterile supermarkets or flourescent convenience stores, impersonal stainless steel and tile. The cottage store was an adventure, a place that carried the personal stamp of its owner and it's environment. It was, for the boy, a step back in time.

He breathed in the pungent coal-smell of the freshly oiled wooden floor. The walls were lined with white-painted plywood shelves and an island four levels high ran down the middle of the store. Everyday items like bread and cereal, soap and cookies shared space with more "cottage-specific" goods like mosquito coils, insect repellant and cans of kerosene. The refrigerator the woman was now cleaning held milk and butter, eggs and cheese. It's neighbour kept bacon and pre-packaged cold-cuts cold while in the crisper drawer, Styrofoam containers held wriggling dew-worms, live bait.

The wall next to the door was hung with a bulletin board full of notices advertising pot luck church suppers, fishing derbies and area businesses. Handwritten signs offered "For Sale: Wooden Rowboat", "Chainsaw, like new, needs carburetor" and "Free, to a good home . . . "

Beside the cork board, a government survey map was tacked to the wall. On it was an outline of the lake, the numbered building lots personalized with the handwritten names of the owners. The boy always took time to locate his grandfather's name, feeling a vicarious thrill of ownership. He was also slightly dismayed to see the number of names that had been pencilled in since last year. The lake was certainly getting crowded; five miles long with over sixty miles of shoreline, over half of the lots were now spoken for.

The old man walked around the store, making his selections and placing them in a cardboard box he held in the crook of his left arm.

The boy meanwhile rotated the comic book rack, carefully considering his options. He already had the new *Archie*, *Bugs Bunny* was definitely too young and *Batman* was getting a little too weird. He had narrowed his choices down to *Kid Colt* or *Rawhide Kid* when his grandfather came up beside him.

"You pick one yet", he asked.

"I don't know. They both look good."

The old man looked at the choices. " Tell ya' what. You get the *Kid Colt* and I'll get the *Rawhide Kid*. Then we'll swap."

The boy looked up and grinned.

"What'll Nana say when she finds out you bought a comic book?'

"Who says she has'ta know?"

They both laughed conspiratorially.

The old man unloaded the box on the glass and oak display case that served as a checkout counter. Marjorie began tallying up the purchases, not even looking at the price tags. She knew how much everything in the store was worth. She worked her way through marshmallows, potato chips, wooden matches and a can of 3-in-1 machine oil, a pound of bacon, a dozen eggs and a box of butter tarts. The boy selected five cellophane wrapped caramel cubes from the open wooden candy tray and added to these five black jaw-breakers for his sister. Marjorie put the penny candy in a small paper sack and folded the top over.

"Will that be all?" she asked.

The old man put the two comic books on the counter.

"These as well. Oh, and a bag of charcoal, the briquet kind. And I got some gas, too."

Marjorie rapped on the window. Outside the teen had finished pumping the gas and had returned to the snowmobile. He raised his head, then held up six fingers.

"I guess that'll be all" he finally said.

"Don't forget about the Coke" the boy reminded him.

"Oh for . . . that's what I came in here for in the first place." Marjorie cackled. "They say the mind's the first thing to go."

The boy returned and put the big bottles on the counter. Marjorie added them to the total and wedged them into the box.

The old man paid her and scooped up his change off the rubber-nibbed coin mat. He handed the box to the boy and picked up the bag of charcoal.

"Take it easy, Marjorie. We'll see ya' later."

"Yup, thanks for comin' in."

The old man held the door for the boy.

"Just put the box in the back seat, okay?" he said.

"Okay" the boy headed toward the car.

The old man dropped a coin in the round-topped pop machine outside the door. He opened the long thin glass door and pulled out a cold bottle of Orange Crush. It immediately began sweating in the heat. He wedged the cap into the bottle opener on the front of the machine and snapped it off. A wisp of cold, carbonated air escaped from the neck. He carried the bottle over to where the teenage gas jockey now sat on an upturned milk crate, probing inside a carburetor with a yellow-handled screw-driver.

"You look like you could use a break." The old man handed the bottle to the teen.

"You know it" he answered. He took the pop and swallowed a large swig. His exhaustion was audible. "Thanks a lot. I needed that," he smiled

"Windshield looks good, I appreciate it."

"No problem. Thanks again for the pop."

The old man smiled and nodded. "Well, take 'er easy. Don't work too hard." He turned and started back to the car.

"Never do", the teen answered. *Nice old guy,* he said to himself. He took another pull from the bottle. *I wonder how he knew I need this.*

The old man's brother pulled into the cottage just after lunch, the brand-new midnight-blue Cadillac crunching to a stop in the gravel driveway. He pushed the automatic trunk release and stepped out of the air-conditioned interior, immediately breaking into a sweat in the afternoon heat.

"Nice car," the old man hollered as he came up from the cottage to greet him. "Looks like a goddamn hearse."

"Now, be nice or I won't let you ride in it", his brother grinned. "How 'ya doin', anyway?"

"Good, good. You?"

"Can't complain. Not that it'd do any good, anyways."

The old man was bare-chested above shapeless old jeans. His brother was wearing a pastel- blue Banlon golf shirt tucked into navy Bermuda shorts. Navy knee hose were set off by white loafers that matched his belt.

His wife got out of the passenger side of the car, a lime green pant suit fighting for attention with her dyed orange hair. On high-heeled sandals, she tottered across the soft gravel and kissed the old man on the cheek.

"How are you, dear?" she asked.

"Fine, fine"

"Good. Well, I have to get into the cottage before I get eaten alive." She waved a manicured hand furiously around her head. Her hairspray, make-up and perfume combined to attract every mosquito in the vicinity.

The old man grinned at his brother, who shook his head in amused disgust. They each grabbed a suitcase from the trunk of the car and headed down the path to the cottage.

"Get'ya a drink?"

"I wouldn't say 'No'"

The old man poured an ounce and a half of substitute 'Canadian Club' into a glass of ice and topped it up with Coke. Into his own glass went a full shot of Black Velvet and an equal amount of water. He couldn't bear the taste of the slop he passed off on his brother as Canadian Club. He stirred both drinks with a fork, the ice cubes tinkling dully as they swirled. He handed his brother his drink, then raised his own glass.

"Old times" he said.

"Old times"

They drank.

"Goddamn, that's good rye. Nothing like Canadian Club."

"Nope, *nothin'* like Canadian Club," the old man agreed.

The heat of the day held on after sundown, turning the night humid. Mosquitoes swarmed in the heavy air. Four fishermen sat in the small aluminum boat, reeking of bug repellent. The old man sat on the rear bench by the motor. The boy shared the middle seat with his father. The old man's brother was wedged into the bow seat, his rump cushioned on a striped lawn chair pad. Overhead, a ripe yellow moon glowed through the haze. Along the shore, they could hear bats furiously hunting insects. Around them, in the weed-bed, bullfrogs burped their bass-note love songs. From a nearby pine-covered island came the whispery call of a whippoorwill.

They had been fishing minnows all around the weed-bed for over an hour with steady action. Most of the fish were tossed back as being too small. Four swam on the stringer off the rear of the boat. A few minutes ago, the bass starting rising to the surface among the weeds, gurgles and splashes announcing their presence. The fishermen immediately exchanged their minnows for surface plugs and set up a drift through the heart of the bed. The old man and the boy's father retrieved skirted yellow Hula Poppers. The boy snapped on a black Jitterbug while Alex fished a silver painted Crazy Crawler. The bass did not seem particular.

The boy's father drew the first strike, the fish rising to the bubbling lure with the speed and impact of a freight train, it's attack driving it clear out of the water. He instinctively jerked the rod tip high over his as the fish returned to the water, intent on finding deep cover. Instead, it felt a sting as the plug's rear gang of treble hooks drove deep into it's jaw. It continued to bulldog it's way into the weeds, but the man pumped the rod, reeling in line at the same time, turning the fish with each pull. Time and again it fought, gathering itself to deliver short bursts of flight.

The fish began to tire now and, seeking to relieved the constant pressure of the hooks, turned toward the boat, rising as it did so. The man hurriedly took up the slack. Twenty feet from the boat, the fish exploded through the surface, furiously shaking its head, trying to throw the hooks loose. With gills flared, it tail-walked across the water, jewelled droplets flying away from it's twisting body. Then, with a flat splash, it re-entered the water, it's energy now almost spent. The man had been able to maintain steady pressure on the line during the fish's aerial acrobatics, preventing it from spitting the lure. He now drew the fish alongside the boat, his rod bent almost double. The fish made a frantic final bid for freedom: twisting, panic-stricken, seeking to overcome exhaustion in a desperate dive for deep water. The man leaned back, fighting off the attempt. Succumbing to the inevitible, the fish finally rose one last time to the surface. The boy, reaching around his father, slipped the aluminum rim of the landing net over the fish and lifted it from the water, ensnared in the green cotton mesh. It gave a few last twitches, then lay still.

"Nice fish", the old man said. "Bet she does close to three pounds."

"It felt more like three hundred when I was trying to turn it away from those weeds." His shoulders were trembling and his wrists and forearms ached. The six minute battle had been intense. A film of sweat had formed on his body during the fight and was now evaporating in the night air, chilling him.

The old man gripped the fish by it's bottom lip. He worked the hooks free and extended it into the air, inspecting the slab-sided body by flashlight; the black back, the olive-green sides shading into bronze and finally to creamy white on the belly, black stripes in a camouflage pattern along it's length. He snapped it onto the stringer and let it settle back into the water.

"Yep, a real nice fish. Nothin' fights like a smallie on the surface", he said.

In the next hour, they landed five more keepers, witnessing one more spectacular airborne display when the old man tied into a tough two pounder.

The night air had cooled now, turning from humid to camp. A heavy dew was forming on the upper surfaces of the boat and frosted the cowling of the motor. They had ten on the stringer when the fish mysteriously quit biting. It was just after midnight and they were clammy and uncomfortable. After a few unanswered casts, they decided to call it a night. The old man hauled their catch aboard and headed for home.

It was two in the morning and old man and his brother faced each other across the kitchen table, playing their sixth game of cribbage. The boy sat between, his eyelids heavy. His father lay on the living room couch asleep, his mouth hanging open.

The old man'd had a run of luck and was leading his brother three games to two, coming back from a two-nothing deficit. Four big hands in a row combined with a streak of nothing hands for his brother put him only five points away from taking the series. To add insult to injury, his brother was still ten holes away from the skunk line and the old man had first count.

He sat back in his chair, a serene look on his face, while Alex hunched over his hand, arranging and re-arranging the cards, searching for a playing hand that would, if not give him victory, at least spare him the embarrassment of a skunking. His frown deepened as he realized it was probably a lost cause.

The old man nudged the boy's leg under the table with his knee and shot him a glance from behind raised eyebrows and half-closed lids. *Needle time.* The old man sniffed the air.

"You smell something'?", he asked as he played a three. The boy sniffed once.

"Whew, somethin' smells around here. What is it?", the old man continued. He tossed a two on his brother's jack. "Fifteen-two." Three points to go. His brother played a nine.

"Twenty four," Alex said flatly.

"Whatever it is, it sure stinks. Is just can't put my finger on it." He slowly fingered his cards, stretching out the agony. He casually flipped a seven on the pile. "Thirty-one for two." He moved his peg, counting "one . . . two" out loud.

"Sonofabitch" his brother said. "You sure got horsehoes up your ass tonight." He slapped down an eight.

"I just can't place it." the old man sniffed again. "Wait a minute, wait . . . a . . . minute. I've got it. I know what it is! It's a *skunk!*" He laid down a seven. "Fifteen-two," He moved his peg into the home spot.

"Sonofabitch." His brother threw his last card down and tossed his useless crib hand in as well.

The old man gathered the cards and began to shuffle them slowly.

"Wanna go again?" he asked with a perfectly straight face. All through the final hand, he had not cracked so much as a smile.

"Go piss up a rope." his brother replied.

"Nice talk in front of the kid," the old man admonished.

"Has anyone ever told you that you're a piss-poor winner?"

"Hundreds of times."

His brother grinned at that. "I'm goin' to bed. Good night."

"See ya' in the mornin'."

"G'night Uncle Alex."

Alex shuffled off to his room. The old man finally allowed himself a chuckle.

"I'm gonna go to bed myself", he said. "You should, too."

The boy yawned. "Yeah, I guess so. G'night, Papa." He got up and headed to bed, pausing on the way to cover his sleeping father with an afghan.

The old man watched, shuffling the cards mechanically, and smiled. *He's growing into a fine young man*, he thought. *Even if he could use a haircut.* He got up and put the deck of cards and the cribbage board on the top of the refrigerator. Picking up the glasses from the table, he took them over to the sink and dumped out what remained of the ice cubes. He put the empty glasses on the countertop and flipped out the kitchen light.

He stood for a while in the darkness, not yet willing to end such a perfect day. Finally, he started for his room.

As he undressed, he chuckled again at the thought of the skunking.

"He never could stand to lose", he said to himself. He slipped between the sheets.

While he slept, he dreamt of fishing for skunks from inside a floating Cadillac.

CHAPTER 6

Tuesday morning had dawned dull and grey, much milder than the day before. A misty drizzle that darkened the pavement and ate into the snow banks added to the gloom.

The young man awoke slowly, rolling over and pulling the comforter up around his face. Finally, he came to terms with the fact that he was awake. He reached across the bed but found only rumpled sheets. His wife must already be up. He scrounged the sleep from his eyes with a thumb and forefinger, kneading the bridge of his nose as he did so. His wife came into the bedroom, towelling her freshly washed hair.

"Oh, you're awake." she said.

His reply came out as a croak. He cleared his throat and tried again.

"Yeah. What time is it?" he raised himself up on his elbows into a sitting position. The numbers on the clock radio were a red blur without his glasses.

"Quarter to eight," his wife told him. "Why don't you try to go back to sleep?"

"Naw, I'm already up."

His wife wrapped the towel, turban-like, around her head and re-tied the belt on her white terry cloth robe.

"I'll put the kettle on for you then." She paused at the bedroom door. "How are you anyway?"

"Fine," he answered automatically. Then he became aware of the genuine concern contained in this usually off-hand question. He looked into his wife's dark worried eyes. He forced a smile.

"Fine," he repeated. "Really."

She nodded and left the room.

He swung his feet out of bed and sat on the edge of the mat-tress. He sighed and scratched the hair on his chest, his tired brain working to sort the errands of the day.

He had to pick up his suit from the cleaners where his wife had dropped it off yesterday. His white dress shirt hung down-stairs in the laundry room, waiting to be ironed. He spied his dress shoes on the floor of the open closet, a layer of dust coating the toes. The young man didn't dress up very often. He made a mental note to put a fresh shine on them. He stood up and stepped into a pair of jeans that lay crumpled on the floor, pulling them up and buttoning the fly. He slipped on a flannel shirt and ran his fingers through his hair. *Maybe get a haircut if there's time.* The thought brought a smile to his face as he remembered the way his grandfather had badgered him about his long hair, going so far as to occasionally refer to him as his "granddaughter." The old man would be tickled to know that the boy was considering a trip to the barber in his honour. The young man put on his glasses and followed the sound of the whistling tea kettle to the kitchen.

* * *

The Pontiac hummed north along the highway, the old man leaning back in the driver's seat. His right wrist hanging over the top of the steering wheel, the middle finger of his left hand hooked on the bottom, making minor adjustments as the road dipped and rose.

The rain clouds of earlier in the day were moving off now, breaking up and allowing huge patches of deep blue sky to show through. The brightness of the late afternoon turned the fleeing storm clouds to dark gun-metal and the trees along the roadside were showing off their full fall splendour, bright golden yellow, burnt oranges and deep fiery reds glowed as though lit with their own inner suns. Long shadows stretched across the highway, dap-pling the asphalt in a wondrous chiaroscuro of bright sunlight and deep shade, an effect intensified by the darkness of the still wet pavement. Each breath of breeze sent a flurry of golden birch leaves fluttering from the trees to the road, only to be picked up again in a whirling, colourful dance in the wake of the passing automobile. Until a few moments before, a faint rainbow had arced over the multi-hued eastern hills.

The old man slowed the car as they entered the limits of the small village. A few houses now dotted the roadside, close enough together to be considered a community. They passed a lumber yard and a Mercury Marine dealership. Coming to a bridge with an arched steel superstructure, they crossed over a churning river, white foam against water a deep Prussian blue. In the passenger seat, the boy's grandmother closed her eyes. She knew it was safe, but still she hated crossing bridges. In the back seat, the boy looked casually out the side window, needing all the thirteen-year-old 'cool' he could muster to disguise the childish thrill he still felt when driving over the rushing water. His grandfather calmly continued to whistle "Don't Fence Me In."

The car thumped over the last expansion joint on the bridge and they found themselves in the downtown core of the small town, two- and three-story buildings with brick facades stretching along both sides of the road for three blocks. The old man angle parked in front of the red brick town hall with its copper-domed clock tower and the community bulletin board out front.

"Okay," said the old man as his wife gathered up her purse and jacket, "we'll meet you back here in twenty minutes." She got out and headed for the IGA.

The old man and the boy started north up the sidewalk toward the hardware store, passing in succession a variety store, a Chinese restaurant and the small-town movie theatre, a poster advertising "Airport '75" as the coming attraction. They stepped up onto the cement stoop and the boy pulled the door open, holding it for his grandfather.

Inside, a man in his late-thirties, his belly hanging comfortably over his belt, was counting bolts. His dark hair was slicked back with Brylcreem, the back woven into a thick ducktail. He had worn it this way since 1955.

That same year he had starred on the local midget hockey team that had won the regional championship. The town had gotten together and presented the whole club with dark-green melton jackets with leather sleeves and filled two buses when the team travelled all the way to Toronto to play on a Sunday afternoon in Maple Leaf Gardens. They put up a good fight but were trounced by a big city team who wore matching stockings and whose sweaters were not full of holes.

It was a long, cold bus ride back home that night and his girlfriend sought a way to console him after the loss. Under a grey wool blanket on the back bench of the rented yellow bus, they huddled together for warmth. Huddling led to cuddling. Cuddling led to kissing. Kissing led to petting and petting led to a wedding one week after graduation that spring. Five months later, his wife presented him with a nine pound-five ounce baby boy, only four months premature. Their son would be attending Boston College in the fall on a hockey scholarship.

He had come to work with his father in the hardware store and took it over five years ago when his old man had run off to Arizona with the cashier from the drug store across the street.

The old man loved hardware stores. He could spend hours browsing through the bins and shelves and baskets. Today, however, he was hunting for a specific item. All summer, a connection on the water pump had been leaking steadily. No amount of tightening, plumbers putty or cursing had stopped it. There was no getting around it: he would have to install a new ring-seal. He began his search, the boy following along.

The old man lifted a pair of huge tin snips off a pegboard rack and scissored the blades loudly.

"Why dont'cha let me give ya' a little haircut, eh? Then maybe ya' wouldn't look like a girl," he said to the boy.

The boy's hair had gotten quite long, covering his ears and

curling over his collar at the back, reaching almost to his shoulders. He wore it parted down the centre and the bangs fell into his eyebrows. He had recently begun using his mother's blow dryer, a fact he wisely kept from his grandfather.

The old man continued. "A little off the top, a little off the sides. A lot off the back. Ya'd look almost normal," he laughed. Although not understanding the running joke, the pompadoured hardware man joined in the laughter anyway.

"You're just jealous because I've got hair," the boy shot back. The old man had recently begun combing his hair straight back from his forehead in an uncharacteristically vain attempt at hiding a rapidly balding crown. As for the hardware man, the boy ignored his laughter, figuring his greased-back 'do made enough fun of itself.

The old man, though stung by the boy's retort, smirked at the comeback. "Smart ass," he grinned, putting the shears back on their hook.

They continued to stroll the aisles, the old man occasionally stopping to add another selection to the growing pile in the boy's arms. The items were nothing he needed, he was merely stocking up against some perceived future hardware emergency. Glass fuses, black electrical tape, a box of brass cup hooks, eighteen feet of marine rope and a half pound of 3" galvanized spiral nails. When he came to the washers, however, he was confronted with a dilemma. He had never actually measured the size of the seal he needed and there was absolutely no way in hell he would ever ask for help. He quickly narrowed his choices down to four packages. One of them has to be the right size, he figured. He picked up the four blister packs and headed for the cash register. The boy tactfully decided not to notice and followed him to the front of the store.

They placed the goods on the counter and the hardware man began to ring up the purchases. Behind him, an eight-year-old Export "A" calendar hung on the wall. The last Toronto Maple Leafs team to win the Stanley Cup smiled at the camera, their royal blue sweaters looking old fashioned, an effect doubled by the short hair worn by the players. Allan Stanley had visited this very hardware store once, and had scrawled his autograph across the top of the photo, adding "Best Wishes" and "#26". Tacked to the wall beside the calendar was a yellow and green chenille hockey crest from 1955. The year the midget hockey team almost went all the way, and at least one of it's defencemen had.

The boy's grandmother was waiting for them in the car when they got back. One look at the two bags told her that her husband had gone on another hardware spree. The boy and the old man were laughing. In a last effort to start something, the hardware man had mentioned as they left that the barbershop was just down the street, guffawing at his own attempt at humour.

The old man had replied with a polite chuckle while the boy forced a grin and rolled his eyes.

Once outside, the boy said "I guess I could buy a couple of cans of 10-W-30 and wear my hair like his."

The old man nodded. "You could also shave yer' butt and walk backwards, but I wouldn't recommend it." He ruffled the boys hair and they walked off toward the car.

The Saturday morning of the Thanksgiving weekend had broken crisp and clear, glittering beneath a rime of frost. Ice had formed along the shoreline in thin glassy wafers. Already, two flocks of geese had honked overhead in a wavering arrow pointing the way south.

Inside, everyone was up and dressed, the boy's parents and sister having arrived late the night before. They sat around the kitchen table, mopping up egg yolk with pieces of toast, dabbing at the few remaining bacon crumbs left on their plates. Second and third cups of coffee and tea fortified them for the day's work ahead; raking the leaves that covered the cottage lot in a dense mat. Although the back and west side of the lot was left natural, the activity area to the east as well as the paths and the driveway had to be cleared. If left, the wet leaves would provide treacherous footing all winter as well as a breeding ground for mosquitoes come spring.

"Well, those leaves aren't gonna rake themselves," the boy's father declared. He rose from the table and drained the last mouthful of coffee from his cup. The boy and the old man agreed and the three men reached for jackets and boots. The women would tidy the kitchen, then join the men outside.

The old man picked up a split-bamboo rake and, walking up the hill, began to gather the leaves from the path that led from the parking area to the cottage.

The boy and his father retrieved two sprung-steel lawn rakes from inside the outhouse and began on the open side yard. Starting at opposite ends, they raked in a line toward one another, meeting in the middle, then retreating to their opposite corners to begin the next row.

The first time the two met in the middle, they ignored one another and returned in silence. The second time they exchanged exaggerated puffs of exertion. The third time in, the boy's father stopped before the boy did and stepped back, watching the boy work. He saw the concentration, the intent of doing a good job. Suddenly, it was if he was seeing his son for the first time as something other than a little boy. His son was becoming a young man. His father wondered when that had happened.

He knew he had been distracted lately, trying to sort out his own life. Perhaps he wasn't paying enough attention to the boy. It's just that he would be thirty-six- years old next month and he realized that this was it. This was his life. He was, right now, living his future. True, he had a fine wife and after fourteen years of marriage, they still loved one another, albeit in a more comfortable, less passionate way. They had been blessed with two fine, healthy, bright children who gave them no cause for worry. They lived in a nice home in a nice neighbourhood and were collecting all the toys of middle-class success. He had no cause to feel the way he did. That, perhaps more than anything caused him the greatest concern. He lit a cigarette and a voice in his head softly spoke. *Don't let him become a stranger.* He inhaled deeply, holding the smoke in his lungs, feeling it's calming effect. Slowly he blew it out in a blue-white vapour. The boy had finished the row.

"You're doin' a good job," the boy's father said.

"Thanks." The comment took the boy by surprise. His father didn't usually offer very many unsolicited compliments, certainly not for something as trivial as raking leaves. "Nice day for it." He made the observation as an attempt to fuel the flicker of conversation. He, too, had missed time spent with his father.

The man had a million questions for his son. *How are you really doing? Who are your friends? What do you want to be? Who are you? Can I help?*

The boy walked back to the end of the row. Behind him he heard his father's footsteps rustling the leaves. He turned to find his father right beside him. He turned to look at him.

"You warm enough , Butch?" his father asked.

He had not been called that by his father in a long while. It had been a nickname for him used solely by his dad when the boy was younger and it had made him feel special, grown up. He didn't notice when exactly it had stopped, didn't realize in fact that it had until his father used it just now.

They began to rake again, only now side by side.

When he was thirteen, the boy's father had dreams of being a major league baseball player. And not just any major league team would be good enough. He would be a Brooklyn Dodger. After all, Gil Hodges couldn't last forever. He was a hot-shot south-paw first baseman. A little big for his age, he routinely played against teams of players three and four years older than himself. Although he could hit with decent power, he was most dangerous as a spray hitter, quick wrists and exceptional hand-eye co-ordination racking up singles and doubles at an almost .500 rate. At fifteen he had led the league in average and RBI's. A sixteen he anchored the Eastern Ontario champs and led both teams in batting and stolen bases before his team lost the All-Ontario's in a bitterly contested seven-game series. The following spring the major leagues came knocking. Not the Dodgers, but the Detroit Tigers. He was invited to a scouting camp along with a handful of other small-town hopefuls. But it was while standing with the other first basemen that he first noticed something. At thirteen, he had been five feet, seven inches tall and towered over most of his teammates. At seventeen, he had stretched all the way to five-seven and a half and was the shortest player in camp. Even the lowly Tigers had no place in the organization for a five-foot-seven-and-a-half inch first baseman. The way their infielders threw, a Tiger first sacker needed all the height and reach he could get.

He returned home and accepted an invitation to play for a new juvenile team being put together in his hometown. He quit after a tournament one month into the season. Along with two other players, he grew tired of being benched in favour of friends of sponsors' sons. Fed up, he left and immediately signed on with a rough and tumble senior team, helping them to another Eastern Provincial title.

He realized, however, that for him sports was destined to be nothing more than a past-time. The following summer, he played only on pick-up tournament teams, pocketing a few bucks here and there, his share of the prize money.

The following spring, he finished high school and set out to make something of himself. He was an intelligent young man with a self-confidence beyond his years. A month after graduation, he accepted a junior management position with a local foundry. The job came with a shirt and tie, a leather briefcase, a cubicle office of frosted glass and oak panelling and a shared secretary. The job also came with a pitifully small pay envelope, half of which he handed over to his mother as room and board.

That fall, his father suffered a series of heart attacks, four within the space of two weeks, the last one finally killing him. He mourned out of a sense of duty, a mask of stony sadness belying an indifferent heart. His relationship with his father had been one of con-

stant criticism, threats and drunken violence. He could not remember his father hugging him, playing catch with him or holding his hand. The only times his father talked to him was to scold
and belittle, disparage and condemn. Looking at his father's face,
judgmental and damning even in death, he knew that was he ever
to have a son, he would be a different kind of father. Much different. He had turned away from his father's face and walked outside
into the golden sunlight of Indian summer and lit a cigarette.

Three years later, he was married with a nine-month-old son
of his own and a cramped two-bedroom apartment. His pay packet
had not increased in over two years. Christmas would be tight,
only enough to get something for the boy. He and his wife would
exchange kisses and a card.

He loosened his executive tie and sat down at the kitchen table.
His wife placed his dinner in front of him. Creamed peas on toast.
Maybe next week he could afford meat.

"You're late tonight," his wife said. "Is everything all right?"

"Yeah. They . . . uh . . . they're hiring at the Motors. I stopped
in on the way home and put in an application."

The "Motors" was the local automobile factory, the city's larg-
est employer. The men of both their families had worked there or
still did. It was hot, hard, heavy manual labour, mind-numbingly
boring. In order to entice a responsible workforce, however, they
paid a good wage and provided a decent benefit package. The man
was preparing to sell his dreams in exchange for a more comfortable life for his family. For the next thirty years, he would be awake
before dawn to stand on his feet for eight long hours a day. On
night-shift, he wouldn't stumble home, dead tired, until almost
three in the morning. He traded his briefcase for a tin lunch bucket
and his pride in a shirt and tie for a larger paycheck. Within two
years, he had moved his wife and son into a three-bedroom brick
story-and-a-half with a huge backyard where one day he would
teach the boy to throw and catch. He turned the third bedroom
into a nursery for their new daughter.

The years since had been spent working and raising the family. He coached his son's softball and hockey teams while his wife taught Sunday school and volunteered as a Brownie and Guide leader. Eventually, they moved to a new home and bought a new car. And every day he picked up his lunch pail and went off to a job he hated.

Lately, though, he had been dreaming, fantasizing, about another life. A life without a mortgage, without a wife and kids, without the boring job on the assembly line that steadily destroyed his sense of self-worth. In his mind, he became a swinging bachelor, some days the major leaguer he dreamt of being years ago, at thirty-five still able to lead his team to the World Series, once again being voted MVP, while on days when his aching knees reminded him of his age, he would be a recently-retired star, putting his vast knowledge to work as a brilliant manager, outsmarting the likes of Sparky Anderson and Walter Alston.

No matter how he earned his six-figure salary, he had plenty of free time to lounge around his modern, Mediterranean-influenced pad; Teak tables and a round bed with a fur bed-spread.

In reality, he settled for growing his sideburns a little longer.

One day, however, as he watched the half-built cars roll by him, he discovered that he was unable to conjure up the fantasy he had created for himself. No matter how hard he tried, he couldn't escape from the fact that he was what he was, a blue collar family man growing increasingly bitter and distant while slugging away at a dead-end job. He subsequently grew more despondent and touchy, unable to find little joy in his home and family.

Three weeks before the Thanksgiving weekend, he awoke at a quarter past five in the morning and stumbled into the bathroom, his eyes fighting to adjust to the sudden brightness of the overhead light. He turned on the hot water faucet and held his hands under the stream, allowing the heat to relieve the stiffness in his fingers. Finally, he splashed water on his face, rubbing the numb sleepiness from his eyes. He looked in the mirror and a terrifying chill washed over him, a cold sweat itching across his back. The face in the mirror was recognizable. But it was not his. He had become what he feared. In front of him, water dripping from a stubble-covered chin, stood his father, glaring back at him.

He spent the rest of the day lost in a blind panic that soon gave way to a determination to change. The decision was easy. The thought of putting it in motion scared the hell out of him.

His wife understood when he told her that night how sorry he was for the way he had been acting lately. She held him, while he cried for the first time since he was a child.

For the rest of the week, he tried to be more pleasant. His daughter came around quickly, eagerly showing him her schoolwork, basking in his rusty attempts at approval.

Things were improving. He was finding a certain pride in being a good family man, a certain nobility in the role of father/provider. Each day, he went off to work with the self-satisfied zeal of a martyr to responsibility. Still, he felt underlying uneasiness. Nothing in his own experience had taught him how to relate as a father to a boy about to become a young man.

When the boy was small, it had been easier. His father could take him to a hockey game or fastball match and be a hero in exchange for a hot dog or a bag of ships. A pack of hockey cards made up for volumes of unspoken "I love you's". But the boy was no longer small. What the man now had to do would require words. And the right moment to deliver them. He never imagined it would come while raking leaves.

"What's this on your lip?" His father reached out a gloved finger and brushed at the boy's top lip. At least a dozen fine dark hairs shadowed the corners of the boy's mouth.

The boy ducked away, grinning with embarrassment and pride. He had wondered how long it would take before someone noticed his, well let's face it, his *moustache*. He was equally proud of wisps of hair sprouting elsewhere on his body. But his upper lip, he could share with the world.

"Comin' in pretty good," his dad continued. "If you want, my razor and shaving cream are in the bathroom. You might want to clean that up before dinner. Of course the more you shave, the thicker it gets," he added, noting with satisfaction that this last comment had the desired effect on the boy, who was already imagining a full, dark beard by Christmas.

They talked of many things that afternoon, nothing earth-shattering, just casual chatter, easy and familiar, the kind of talk that is shared by friends, by men. The boy noticed the change in tone. He recognized it from hours spent listening to his father talk to other men while standing along the rail at the local arena or on the top bench of the bleachers at some dusty ballpark, while he sat seen, but not heard. He slowly adapted to the elevation in status conferred upon him by his father, not quite sure how to respond at first, growing more comfortable as he recognized his father's earnestness.

It took them nearly twice as long as it should have to rake the side yard. By the time they finished, the old man had started burning the pile of leaves he had gathered. The boy's grandmother tended the fire, turning and stirring the leaves and twigs with a garden rake. His mother and sister finished sweeping the deck and began carrying bushel baskets of leaves to the burnsite.

The old man watched his son-in-law and the boy. Normally steady, hard workers, he had seen them pausing often, leaning on their rakes, talking instead of working. He was about to tease them, calling them lazy and kidding about letting him do all the work. Then he noticed the expressions of respect, attentiveness and something he could only define as relief on their faces and in their manner. He saw a father and son enjoying each other's company, the boy animatedly describing some schoolyard adventure, the father now showing his son how to hold a rake using his fingers instead of his palms, keeping his thumbs pointing up on the handle instead of wrapping them around, avoiding blisters. He had noticed the previous distance between the two and was glad to see them talking so easily. He left them alone.

The boy and his father finished their raking and began bringing the leaves to the fire. The old man took over the tending chores from his wife and the women went into the cottage to prepare dinner.

The Thanksgiving turkey had been in the oven since midmorning and would soon be ready. The boy's mother began peeling potatoes, her daughter went to work on a bag of carrots. His grandmother began setting the table.

Outside, the two men and the boy fed leaves to the fire, turning the pile steadily to allow oxygen to reach the flames. They circled constantly, avoiding the thick, white smoke shifting with the breeze, acrid and toasty-smelling. It was a perfect fall day, a perfect Thanksgiving.

The kitchen was warm when they entered, cheeks and ears pink from the frosty air outside. The temperature had begun dropping rapidly as the sun sank toward the trees that lined the western shore. They hung their coats on the brass hooks just inside the door and pulled off their work boots. The savoury smell of roast turkey and sage dressing filled the cottage and they breathed deeply, almost tasting the delicious odour. Their stomachs growled in anticipation of the feast, a combination of hard work and fresh, cold air making them ravenous.

The women had been working on the meal for most of the afternoon, tasting each dish, adding a pinch of this and dash of that, tasting again to measure the improvement.

The men had just enough time to wash before dinner. Already the turkey sat on the table, it's skin basted a rich crispy chestnut. A piece of tin foil lay over top, keeping in the heat and juices.

The old man and the boy's father quickly scrubbed the dirt and ashes that smudged their hands and faces, towelling dry briskly. The boy took a little longer and when he sat down at the table next to his father, the man caught the familiar whiff of Gillette Foamy and saw that the boy had taken him up on his offer of the use of his razor. He felt a strange surge of pride, as he realized the boy had just crossed some invisible threshold, rising to another rung on the ladder toward manhood.

The boy caught his father staring at his upper lip, the man shooting him a quick wink. He fought to suppress a self-conscious grin while he blushed pink.

Everyone else was too concerned with Thanksgiving dinner to notice the evidence of the boy's recent rite of passage. Plates began to pile with slices of white turkey, clear juices attesting to its moist perfection. Potato dressing, full of bread, onions and sage had been baked inside the bird and was now being spooned out of a bowl and onto the plate of the old man. Honey glazed carrots, crisp green beans, snow white potatoes whipped with milk and butter, turnip mashed with an egg and brown sugar; it was all hungrily being divvied up on plates around the table.

"Wait, wait, wait. Wait a minute." The boy's mother interrupted the feeding frenzy. "It's Thanksgiving. I think we all have *something* to be thankful for." She looked at her husband, who looked at the boy. The boy felt the soft bristles at the corner of his mouth with the tip of his tongue.

"Let's drop our forks, bow our heads and say grace," his mother suggested. "Dad, would you lead us?"

The old man stopped short, a forkful of potatoes hovering in front of his open mouth. He closed his lips, still eyeing the food. Finally he sighed and lowered the fork to his plate. He clasped his hands in front of him, closed his eyes and lowered his head. Around the table the others followed suit.

"Over the lips, over the gums, look out . . ."

"Dad!" The boy's mother stopped him, then shot a disapproving glare at her giggling children, stifling them.

"Okay, okay," the old man said. He'd had his fun and was now ready to talk to God. He composed his face, sombrely becoming a puritan preacher before their eyes.

"Our father, once again we are fortunate to gather together in your presence to thank you for the many blessings you have sent our way. We thank you, as well, for the food we are about to eat, mindful of those who must do without. Please cast your grace upon them. Amen."

Around the table came an answering "Amen."

"Thank you, Dad," the boy's mother said softly. Reaching out and gently squeezing his forearm.

The boy's grandmother, swept up in the emotion of the moment, spoke up. "I have an idea: let's all take turns sharing something that we are thankful for. We should join hands, too."

"Don't push it," the old man glared at his wife. "You all got your grace and that's enough. Now somebody pass me the goddamn pickle tray."

"Now, *there's* something to be thankful for," said the boy's father. "Amen."

The boy was helping himself to more turkey and dressing when he felt his mother's eyes on him, studying his face. A small scab of dried blood just to the right of his mouth had caught her attention. The boy tried to ignore her.

"How did you cut your face?" she finally asked.

Shit, thought the boy. Beside him, he felt his father stiffen. There was no way he couldn't answer.

"Shaving," he said as nonchalantly as possible, dropping another slice of white meat onto his plate.

"Oh!," his mother exclaimed, feeling the boy's embarrassment, sorry she had asked. Her husband sat working a non-existent piece of turkey from between his front teeth with his tongue. For a moment she wished she could bite her's off.

Everyone felt the boy's discomfort and were willing to let the whole subject drop. Everyone except the boy's sister.

"*Shaved!*" she blurted. "You shaved?" She twisted in her seat, craning her neck for a better look. "Why?" she finally asked.

Her brother remained silent, ignoring her, trying to preserve his dignity.

"Be quiet and eat," her mother admonished.

"But, he shaved his face. I don't know why he had to . . . Ow!"

She glared at her mother who, beneath the table, had just delivered a sharp kick that caught the girl just below the kneecap.

"Eat your carrots, they're good for you," she said menacingly, smiling through clenched teeth.

"Amen," said the old man around a mouthful of turnip.

After dinner, the three men sat in the living room, pants unbuttoned and zippers at half mast. Occasionally, one would issue a puffing burp following by a slow exhalation of air and a low groan. They gently massaged distended bellies with the flats of their hands, the stupefying effects of too much turkey leaving them inert and heavy-lidded.

The boy's father blew air between his lips. "Why do we do this to ourselves? Every year I say I won't overeat and then I always do. I feel like I'm gonna explode."

"Well, the way I figure it, you never know when you're gonna eat your last Thanksgiving dinner," the old man said. "I'll be damned it I get up from my last one still feeling hungry."

"You're all a bunch of gluttons", the boy's grandmother said. She and her daughter sat on the couch, smug with their gastronomic restraint. The boy's sister lay on her stomach on the floor, doing homework. It hurt the boy to watch her.

"I can't hear the T.V.," the old man said, shutting his wife up. On the screen, Tommy Hunter was joining his guests in a singalong of country standards.

His wife got in a parting shot. "Probably got turkey in your ears." They smiled at one another.

"Well," she said. "Who's ready for a piece of pie? We got apple or pumpkin."

"I'll have pumpkin," the boy's mother said, getting up to help.

"Nothing for me, right yet," said his sister.

The three men looked at each other, sizing up one another's courage and capacity. They knew that to eat anymore would be foolish, if not actually fatal. They would not accept. They would not stoop to making pigs out of themselves. They would not . . .

The thought of apple pie, warm from the oven, spiced with cinnamon, it's crust flaky and light was too much for the boy's father. He held up a hand, the thumb and index finger a few inches apart.

"Maybe just a small piece," he said. "Apple, please."

The old man imagined creamy pumpkin, the hint of nutmeg he always found exotic-tasting and the scoop of vanilla ice cream melting slowly beside the warm wedge.

"What the hell," he said. "Pumpkin, please. With a scoop of ice cream."

The boy hesitated, his stomach already uncomfortably beyond capacity. It was trying to keep up with the two men at dinner that had left him feeling like this. He had nothing to prove.

Just then, his sister looked up at him, her expression one of feigned innocence. "Go ahead," she said to him. "It'll put hair on your chin."

A hateful glare from him sent her head back to her homework, snickering to herself.

"Apple, please," he heard himself say.

You'll pay for this, said his stomach.

CHAPTER 7

The young man stood in his kitchen, ironing one of his two dress shirts. He was wearing a plaid flannel bathrobe over bikini briefs and black dress socks. His wife entered the kitchen and smiled.

"Nice look," she teased, "I wish I had a camera."

"I wish I had a wife who'd iron my shirts," he said, struggling with a cuff.

"Welcome to the 'Eighties," she countered. "How do I look?" His wife was wearing a forest green coat dress with black velvet-covered buttons and a matching collar. Her legs were sheathed in dark nylon stockings and she wore a pair of black velvet pumps. He had given her the etched gold locket and matching earrings just this past Christmas.

"You look great. I bet you're the prettiest girl at the funeral." He had a dark sense of humour at times. He finished the shirt and unplugged the iron. He shrugged out of the robe and pulled on his still-warm shirt. "How's this?," he asked, "better?"

"Just get dressed."

He went to the bedroom and pulled on charcoal gray pleated pants, doing up the black leather belt after carefully tucking in the shirt. He laced on his freshly-polished dress shoes and, standing, checked the break of his pant's cuff. Facing the mirror, he wrapped a deep burgundy silk tie into a sharp four-in-hand, forming a dimple just below the knot, then buttoned down the collar of his white Oxford shirt and slipped on the charcoal-grey double-breasted suit coat. He stared at himself in the mirror and took a deep breath. He was ready to go to his grandfather's funeral.

"You look fine," his wife said quietly from the doorway.

"Thanks. Well, let's go, I guess."

They were meeting his parents and his grandmother at the funeral home at one-thirty, a half-hour before visitation. He and his wife were just stepping out of the car as they pulled in.

His father was first out, opening the back door and helping his mother-in-law out. She stood wearing a look of confusion, tiredness and grief making the events of the last few days unreal and bewildering. The boy's mother had gotten out of the passenger seat and hurried to her mother's side, her own expression of sorrow overlapped with a look of worry for the older woman's fragile state.

They needn't really worry about her though. Although her husband had gone to great lengths to shelter and pamper her, the boy's grandmother was no stranger to the harsh realities of life.

Her father had immigrated to Canada from Great Britain as an infant, just before the turn of the century. He was raised with a love of his adopted home and deep sense of his ancestry. When the Great War exploded in 1914, he rushed to enlist, eager to represent Canada in her defence of Mother England. His military career ended one horrible day near Ypres in a cloud of chlorine gas, as one of the valiant Canadians who held the line while around them, the French broke and retreated. Breathing through a urine-soaked handkerchief, he did his best only to eventually be felled by a lungful of the searing poison. For months after, he coughed up pieces of his blistered lungs. After a long convalescence in England, his lungs finally stopped shedding, though their elasticity was destroyed by scar tissue. For the rest of his life, he would be plagued by breathing difficulties.

The one positive event to come from his injuries was his meeting with a pretty young Irish nurse. Her spirit and smile, her deep emerald eyes and auburn hair captivated him and he set out to win her heart. When he sailed for Canada in the summer of 1919, she sailed with him as his wife. Two years later, the boy's grandmother was born. Four years later, a second daughter was born and two years after that, a third little girl came along. Three days after giving birth to this last child, his wife died of complications. Devastated by the loss of his wife, handicapped by his wounds and unable to secure steady, decent-paying work, he felt he had no choice but to put his daughters up for adoption.

The baby was the first to go. Taken in by a wealthy banker, she was raised in a fine home, surrounded by luxuries she would otherwise never have known.

The middle girl went next with a well-to-do farm couple. She was raised in the country in the heart of a loving family. Eventually she became a nurse.

The boy's grandmother watched her two sisters taken away. When her turn came, she threw a terrible tantrum, kicking the man and biting the woman. They fled without her. Twice more, prospective parents ran in horror from the behaviour of this incorrigible little terror. Finally her father relented and the two faced the world together.

The years that followed were a series of temporary menial jobs and shabby rooming houses, hand-me-down clothes and free time spent, not playing, but cooking and cleaning, ironing and mending, taking care of her father while he tried to earn a living, hampered by his battered lungs. Finally he was able to secure a steady job as a handy man on a horse farm. The owner of this farm was a wealthy businessman who had held the rank of colonel in the Great War and subsequently held a soft spot for returning veterans, particularly those who had been wounded. For the first time, the man and his daughter felt secure and safe.

In a further attempt to provide his daughter with a normal home life, he married a woman only eight years older than the girl. He was not particularly in love with this woman, but she was attractive enough and he thought she would be a suitable companion for the girl.

The girl and her stepmother instantly despised one another. The girl resented the intrusion into the life she shared with her father. The woman was insecure about her place in her new instant family and, as a result, was insanely jealous of any attention her husband gave his daughter. By her position as "lady of the house", the woman held the upper hand on the girl and in intimate moments with her husband, would try to poison his mind against his daughter.

One night, however, at the age of seventeen, the girl's life changed forever. In the company of a school friend, she had attended a dance at a lakeside pavilion. Attractive, with her father's penetrating hazel eyes and her mother's rich auburn hair, she caught the eye of a slender young man with a lopsided grin and a cockiness that she found irresistible. By the second dance, she was in love. By the third, so was he. That night, he walked her home under a perfect star-filled sky, the sweet smell of new spring leaves perfuming the air. They held hands and when he said goodnight, he boldly kissed her cheek.

All that summer, they saw each other whenever they could. Often she visited him at the gas station where he worked, brining him lunch, his favourite cheese and onion sandwiches and a pint bottle of cold buttermilk. At a late August picnic, he proposed marriage and that fall they were wed, moving to a cold water flat above a butcher shop. The Second World War had broken out and he tried to enlist, imagining himself in the handsome blue uniform of the Royal Canadian Air Force. Unfortunately, he was colour blind and was unable to distinguish the blue recruiter's uniform from the green grass outside. They thanked him for his time and sent him on his way.

He took a job in munitions factory, working six days a week, often covering two shifts. He toiled hard, pushing himself to exhaustion, punishing himself for not being in uniform.

A year after they married, their daughter was born. That was the same year he managed to get into the service. He was shipped out to train as a gunner in the Tank Corps.

She moved into the home of her in-laws. After tucking her daughter into bed at night, she went off to work, rivetting landing gear assemblies for Mosquito light bombers.

One day in 1943, he came home on leave. That night as they lay in bed, savouring their closeness, he told her that this would be the last time they would be together for a while. He had volun-

teered for overseas duty and would be shipping out within the
month. She cried then, cursing his impetuousness, angry at him
for willingly putting his life at risk, frightened at the thought of
being left alone to raise the small child sleeping in the next room.
He held her until she finally sobbed herself to sleep.

For the rest of the duration, she worked and saved and raised
their daughter. She wrote to him faithfully once a week and anx-
iously awaited his answering letters. On sunny afternoons, she helped
her father-in-law tend to his victory garden and, after harvest, put up
dozens of mason jars of preserves with her mother-in-law.

On V-E day, she took her daughter downtown and they
laughed and danced and sang and cried. On V-J day, they did it
all over again.

He came home in the spring of 1946. The factory where she
had worked switched from aircraft back to automobiles and soon
she was laid off, replaced by a returning serviceman.

He'd had enough of taking orders and was determined to be
his own boss. They took their life savings and opened a small grocery store. They worked long hours and, at night, would fall into
bed exhausted, yet happy. However, the bills soon began to pile
up. He was a generous man by nature. Generous, in fact, to a
fault, ready to extend credit to anyone who came in with a hard
luck story. His generosity, however, did not impress the banker.
Before long, the store was forced out of business. With it went all
their money. He signed on the graveyard shift at the car plant,
sweeping floors. She found work in the catalogue department at
Eaton's. Together, they paid off their debts and, soon after, managed to put a down payment on a building lot. Over the next two
years, as money and time allowed, they built their home.

Slowly things began to improve. His hard work was recognized and he was promoted to foreman, then to general-foreman.
Her pay cheque increasingly went towards luxury items. Life was
good. No one deserved it more.

* * *

The July morning was shaping up to be a fine summer day, warm without being uncomfortably hot, flocks of soft white clouds moving across the bright blue sky, herded along by a soft breeze. A group of men gathered under the cottage, cool in the shade, holding shovels and pick axes, the old man moved about in front of them, gesturing with sweeping arms, now pausing to mark the dirt with his shovel blade.

"If we dig in from about here," he drew a line in the dirt with his toe, "it oughtta be good enough to give us about an eight foot ceiling after we pour the floor."

All winter, he had planned the new basement. Now they were about to excavate into the slope under the cottage. They would do all the digging by hand.

"Don't know why ya' don't bring in one of them little goddamn bullnosers," commented Ed.

The men grinned and pressed the mouths against the backs of their work gloves. The old man ignored him.

"Now, Marjorie's son-in-law, Bruce, is gonna pour the footings and lay the cinder block walls. I was gonna do it myself, but he quoted me a price that wouldn't have made it worth my while." The old man always felt an explanation was necessary when he hired someone to do work for him. "He says he can get a cement truck in here, so he's gonna float the floor, too."

The men thought about the work involved, heaving cinder blocks, preparing yard after yard of concrete in a portable mixer, bag upon unwieldily bag of cement, countless shovelfuls of sand and gravel. No one argued against the old man's decision to let Bruce bring in a truck.

"So, all we have to do is dig her all out," the old man finished.

The boy's father lowered his shovel blade to the ground. "Well, it isn't gonna dig itself," he said stepping into a load of dirt, lifting it and dropping it into a waiting wheelbarrow. Beside him, the boy began digging. The old man and Ed teamed up to fill a second wheelbarrow, while two more of the old man's friends, Charlie and Fred, worked around a third, exchanging their backs for a few days in cottage country. The first few feet went quite easily, the slope shallow and soft.. The men worked steadily and rhythmically, taking turns making the trips to empty the wheelbarrows. A top layer of soil, about six inches and red-brown in colour soon gave way to hard packed yellow-ochre sand. After two hours of digging, they had made decent headway, the excavation running a little more than three feet into the slope, about waist deep now. The workers went to the dock and, laying flat out on their bellies, splashed cool lake water on their arms, necks and faces, then sat back, water soaking into the collars of their shirts. The man cracked open cold bottles of beer, the boy having to settle for a Coke. After twenty minutes, the old man picked up his shovel.

"Take your time, I'm just gonna pick away at it," he said. Within five minutes, they were all back, hard at work.

Noon hour found them sitting on the dock again, hungrily munching egg salad sandwiches, washing them down with ice tea or beer.

Charlie stretched his neck painfully, groaning, then sighing as it cracked twice.

"Ah . . . that's better. I swore when I got back from Italy that I wouldn't ever touch a goddamn shovel again. I bet I dug my way from one end of that country to the other."

"You were in Italy, were ya', Charlie?" Ed asked.

"Yeah. Nice place when you weren't diggin' slit trenches or gettin' shot at. 'Course in the rainy season, the bloody holes would fill up with mud and water faster than we could dig 'em out."

"I know what you mean," Ed said. "At least about gettin' shot at. We didn't do much diggin' in recon, but there were times when I sure as hell made use of a slit trench or two."

"You in Italy, too?" Charlie asked.

"France," Ed said, "France and Holland. Landed on June 8, D-plus-two, and didn't get back to lovely old England until the goddamn shootin' stopped. Did get to deliver food to the Dutchmen, though. God, I remember them poor bastards. Women, kids, old buggers. Nothin' to eat but horsemeat and tulip bulbs. Geezus Murphy, but they were glad to see us. Germans agreed to a cease-fire an' we drove right through their lines, bringin' 'em truckloads of food. The Krauts even helped us unload. Not a bad bunch of fellas, when they weren't tryin' to kill ya'."

"You were navy, weren't you Fred?" Charlie asked the old man's other friend. He knew Fred "was navy" but he didn't know any details.

"Yeah," said Fred. "Corvette duty in the North Atlantic. Halifax to Liverpool an back. Did the Murmansk run once. Sometimes, I would have given my left nut for a chance to dig in some nice dry dirt."

Ed commiserated. "Yeah, I hear those convoy runs were a real bastard. Goddamn U-boats an' all."

Fred stared into the water lapping gently against the dock. "They'd sneak right into the middle of us. It'd be pitch black out there at night. All of a sudden, there'd be a flash and a ship would go up in flames. A couple minutes later, another one would go. We'd go in to try to pick up survivors. That water was so cold. They wouldn't last more than a few minutes. Oil'd be burnin' on the water, some poor bastards right in the middle of it. We pulled some out, their skin was peelin' right off them. Sometime's I'd think it would have been doin' them a favour to let 'em slip right back into the water." He fell silent. Even now, he still woke up some nights, bathed in a fearful sweat, snapped from his sleep by a distant torpedo blast echoing from deep in his memory. He took a pull from his bottle of beer.

Ed turned to the old man. "You were overseas too, weren't ya'?" he asked.

"Yeah."

"See any action?"

"No." The old man stared at his shoes. "Let's get back to work." He got up and headed up the hill.

The digging was progressing more slowly now as they worked deeper into the slope. They had been forced to switch to a different method now, one man picking at the wall of dirt, loosening it and letting it fall. After a half a dozen swings, he would step back, while his partner scooped up the loose dirt.

The old man had been uncharacteristically quiet since the talk of the war. The others notice and allowed him his space, only casting the occasional curious glance his way.

As they dug farther below the surface, they encountered more and more rocks and, worse, tree roots. The roots could normally be severed with a few chops of a shovel or pick. Now and then, however, they would come across a wrist-thick specimen that would require special attention. The boy and his father were at this moment confronted with just such a super root. The boy looked around for a solution and his eyes fell on the axe that Ed had brought with him.

"Hey, Ed," the boy said. "Can we use your axe for a minute? We got a pretty big root over here."

Ed straightened up slowly, then looked right at the boy.

"I don't know," he finally said, shaking his head. "I'm kinda attached to this axe. It's kinda like an heirloom. Belonged to my grandfather, so it did. He passed it along to my daddy as a weddin' gift and when daddy died, well, it's one of the few things he left me."

They had all stopped working now, surprised at the sentimentality coming from the usually gruff Ed.

Ed looked each one of them in the eye, solemnly, as he cradled the axe in his huge hands.

"Yep, sure would hate to see anything happen to this axe, what with it bein' my granddaddy's and all," he breathed a deep sigh. "Course, it's had three new heads and six new handles."

The men broke up laughing. Even the old man shook off his sombre mood and chuckled. Ed handed the axe to the boy.

"Here, watch ya' don't cut yer goddamn leg off."

In the barbecue, the charcoal had burned down to a heap of light grey ash, shimmers of heat still rising in the cooling evening air.

The cottagers sat on the deck, bellies full of hot dogs, hamburgers and potato salad. Few words passed amongst them. They were content to sit and watch the lake gently ripple, the shadows on the far shore growing deep and dark in the golden twilight. The forest was quiet now, the daylight dwellers seeking burrow and roost, the creatures of the night just beginning to stir. Outside the weedbed, ripples grew in concentric rings as a fish rose to sip a morsel from the surface.

"Well," the old man broke the silence, "I'm going' for a fish. Anybody else wanna come?"

By way of answering, the boy rose and headed for the stairs. Upon reaching the boathouse, he tucked his tackle box under his arm, picking up his grandfather's green steel chest in the same hand. In the other, he held both their rods. When he got to the boat, his grandfather was already pumping the gas line. The boy returned with the life jackets as the motor sputtered to life. He untied the lines, and pushing off from the dock, neatly stepped aboard. His grandfather reversed to deeper water, then shifted the gear lever to forward. The boat picked up speed as it headed out across the lake. The whole procedure had taken place without a single word being exchanged between them.

The old man had travelled by truck from Camp Borden to the Exhibition grounds in Toronto. There, he was billeted in the horse barns of the Coliseum, two cots per stall. Three nights later, he was marched to Union Station where he boarded a troop train rolling east.

As he passed through his hometown just before dawn, he looked out the window and thought of his wife and little girl, sleeping less than a mile away. He wondered when, and indeed if, he would see them again.

They rolled into Brockville just after lunch and changed trains, changing again that evening in Montreal. Sometime the next night, they pulled into Halifax. Within days, he was "somewhere in the North Atlantic", crowded below decks of a heaving ship, fighting to keep down his rations. When they finally reached England, he stumbled ashore like the rest; tired, cramped, weak and suddenly ravenous.

They settled down to train, living in wooden barracks through the wet, cold English winter. Pointless exercises only temporarily relieved the tedium of inaction. The old man looked forward to the nights when he didn't have guard duty. He would walk into a little town, where he would down a few pints, maybe throw some darts or hone his cribbage game. It was while playing crib one night that he met a young Englishman named Percy Whittaker.

"Perce", as he was called, had been invalided out of the service after leaving his left foot behind on the beach at Dunkirk. He had returned home to find that his young wife was not at all bothered by his injury. He also found himself a father to a bright young daughter conceived during his last leave before he went across the Channel. The old man taught him to play crib and, in exchange for the lessons, Perce took him home for dinner. The old man immediately fell in love with this young English family, substituting them for his own far across the ocean. He visited as often as he could.

As winter gave way to spring, England grew giddy in anticipation of the coming invasion. No one, of course, knew the details, but it was coming nonetheless. In early April, the old man learned he was being shipped out of the area. The Whittakers had him over for a final, farewell dinner. After a dinner of fried sausages and chips, Perce announced he was taking the old man down to the pub for one last game of cribbage. His wife kissed the old man's cheek, her eyes glistening. His daughter wrapped her arms tight around his neck, squeezing him hard.

At the pub, they played a few hands of crib and proceeded to get gloriously drunk. As they shook hands for the last time outside the pub, Perce's face grew grave.

"Make sure you make it home to your wife and daughter. It's better to be a live daddy than a dead hero."

The old man tried to be serious, nodding solemnly, then breaking into a drunken giggle. "Thanksh Pershe. I mean it," he quit

grinning. "You've been good to me. I don't know how I ever . . . "
His face collapsed and the tears started, his composure ruined by
the booze.

Perce patted his arm, leaning forward on his crutches. "I know,"
he said softly. "I know." He cleared his throat, "Now, get on back
to camp before they leave for France without you. Go on." He gave
the old man's arm a final pat, then turned and made his way up
the road.

The old man watched him go, took a deep breath and turned,
lurching drunkenly back toward camp.

He had gone about a mile and was singing "Tumblin' Tum-
bleweeds" at the top of his voice. Suddenly, from behind, a Morris
Minor with it's headlights masked in accordance with the black-
out regulations, roared past him. Startled, he jumped into the
shoulder of the road. Underfoot, mud and gravel gave way and the
old man found himself lying in a ditch full of water, icy cold from
the spring run off. He giggled, called out "Help, I'm drowning,"
pulled himself to the side of the ditch and fell asleep, his legs still
in the water.

"Well, to make a long story short, I got complications from double
pneumonia and spent the rest of the war recovering in a London
hospital. I don't think they'll ever make a movie about me."

They had been sitting in the boat for almost an hour, casting
Mepps Black Furys mechanically, more for something to do than
actually trying to catch fish.

Finally the boy retrieved his lure and didn't cast it out again,
only letting it spiral, dripping, on the end of his line. Without
looking at his grandfather, he'd asked , "What happened, during
the war I mean?"

For a while, the old man had said nothing. Then he had told
the boy of waking up, hungover and absent without leave, in a
ditch full of cold water beside an English roadway. Two days later,
he was in a hospital bed, delirious with a raging fever, pneumonia
in both lungs.

"How come you didn't tell that story this afternoon? It's pretty good."

"It's not exactly like I did anything. Dammit, those guys had their lives on the line. They share that. Other than a few buzz bombs that came close, I spent the war safe and snug while they fought the war for me. What did I do to compare with that?"

They fell silent for a moment, staring out at the water.

"You went," the boy finally said. "You went and you were willing. That makes you as much a hero as any of them." He cast out his lure. "As least it does to me."

The old man thought about what the boy had said, glad for the low light of dusk. He cast and began to retrieve, aware of the vibration of the bait's spinner blade. Maybe the boy was right. Maybe it was enough that he had been willing. Undoubtedly, if the war had lasted a little longer, he would have been in the thick of it. After V.E. day, he even volunteered for duty in the Pacific. For the first time since the war had ended, he did not feel ashamed of his service. He made another cast.

"Did I ever tell ya' about this sergeant major I had when I first got to England?" he asked the boy.

"No," smiled the boy "tell me."

By the third day of digging, they were almost finished. Just after noon the day before, the old man's brother had arrived, bringing along Donald, his hulk of a son-in-law.

"Geez, you got a lot of work left to do," Alex had said as soon as he arrived. "Good thing I brought Donald."

The big lummox puffed out his chest causing his chin to tuck into the flesh of his neck. Six-foot-three and two hundred and eighty-three pounds, a T-shirt stretched over the puddle of flesh that melted over his belt, he flexed his beefy arms, working them back and forth, pumping up.

The boy's father took a look and whispered to the boy, "Those aren't chest muscles, they're tits." The boy stifled a laugh against his shoulder.

Meanwhile, Donald hoisted a shovel and adjusted his jeans. In order to accommodate his waist, his pants were actually several sizes too large, the crotch hanging almost to his knees. It didn't help that, in spite of his size, Donald didn't have much of an ass to speak of. He spit on his hands and rubbed them together.

"Stand back," Alex said. "Once Donald gets started, the dirt's gonna fly." Alex was obviously mistaking fat for muscle.

To one side, the boy and his father continued working, steadily making progress into the face of the slope, pacing themselves so that they could work all day without slowing. They took a small break now to watch as Donald attacked the earth.

"He won't last five minutes going like that," commented the boy's father as dirt flew from Donald's shovel in a frenzy of digging. Some of it even ended up in the wheelbarrow. Furiously, he flailed at the slope, the shovel as much a bludgeon as a digging tool. He proved the boy's father wrong though, lasting almost seven minutes before dropping his arms to his sides in exhaustion. Sweat poured from his face, which was flushed an unhealthy red save for the white around his lips. Looking slightly nauseous and blowing like a hard ridden horse, Donald was clearly finished for the time being.

"Take a break son," said Alex, a little embarrassed. "Go on up to the cottage." He began leading his son-in-law away.

"Helluva job, Donald," said Charlie, managing to keep a straight face. Beside him, Fred had to turn away.

"Go sit down before your goddamn head explodes," advised Ed.

The old man just shook his head. "Big dumb ox," he muttered, once his brother had led Donald out of earshot.

Donald wasn't a bad sort. Friendly and honest, he was always willing to lend a hand. As a child, he had been quite bright, able to both read and write by his fourth birthday. Unfortunately, he was also quite overweight. When he started school, the teacher and his classmates automatically labelled him lazy, stupid and worthless. It was not long before Donald accepted their opinion.

Not long after, even he began to believe them, becoming what they judged him to be.

When he started high school, the football coach took one look at his size and recruited him as a lineman. Suddenly Donald was not longer the "fat kid." Now he was an athlete, his bulk working to his advantage. He was still not one of the "in" crowd, but at least when he walked off the field, battered and muddy, his doughy body covered with welts and bruises, he could imagine that some of the cheers were for him. By his second year, he had learned that his worth was based not on what he thought or said or felt, but on what he could do.

Occasionally, however, the bright, inquisitive child that had been locked away deep inside would burst forth. Alex's daughter saw this. She also saw that in spite of the brutish front he hid behind, he had a kind and gentle soul. She set out to nurture this, fanning the spark, hoping it might ignite into flame.

Around her, Donald could be himself, knowing that his thoughts, his feelings, his dreams, would not be laughed at. Away from her side, however, he still lapsed into the lumbering beast of burden he knew the world saw him as; trying to do with his body what they would not allow him to do with his brain.

Donald now sat, spilling out over the webbing of the lawn chair. In the shade of the cottage, his colour was gradually returning to normal. The bitter bile of embarrassment still burned in his throat. Beside him, his wife held a cold cloth to the back of his neck. His left hand was curled into a tight fist and he pounded it slowly and steadily, on the arm of the chair. He could never remember feeling this stupid.

It was mid-afternoon on the third day and they were almost to the back wall. It was warm and stuffy this far under the cottage, the breeze unable to reach them. They worked in silence, their tools rasping into the sandy, gritty soil. The atmosphere was dank and earthy, the musty smell of damp wood adding a certain wildness to the air. And now, something else.

The old man sniffed "Whew, what's that?"

The men all stopped to test the air. A few more shovelfuls from the wall and the smell grew worse. The boy was the first to notice the visual evidence.

"Smells like . . . I don't know what," he said, wrinkling his nose.

A few more minutes work and a dark stain had been unearthed halfway up the wall, a greenish-gray ooze mixing with the dirt. The old man picked at it with the point of his shovel. A lump fell away, landing wetly with a foul plop. He nudged it with his toe. It became clear to him what it was. The seepage. The fetid, sour odour. They all added up to one thing.

"Shit," he said flatly.

"That's what it is," confirmed Ed.

That's what it was, indeed. The septic tank had rotted out, the sheet steel skin corroding away until a hole the size of a dinner plate had appeared in the bottom, allowing the contents to seep into the ground and, now, into the excavation that soon would be the old man's basement. He scraped out a little more of the moist, dark stain.

"Shit," he said again.

The sun beat down on the old man and the boy as they stood staring down at the battleship grey tank that they had spent all morning and most of the afternoon unearthing. They had disconnected the tiles and the main stack running down from the cottage. With the earth removed, the odour wafted up out of the hole, attracting flies intent on a meal. All that now remained to be done was to raise the tank. They were a little short of manpower, the end of holidays taking everyone back to the city. The old man was staying up for an extra week, the boy volunteering to stay to help out as well.

The boy sized up the tank, then looked at the slope it had to got up. "Big job," he finally observed.

"Yeah, well, Stan said he'll lend us a hand. He said we could use his truck and trailer, too." The boy looked doubtfully at the old man who answered with a shrug. "Well, maybe he can drive at least." They both laughed.

Stan had a cottage a few lots up the lake. He didn't like the woods, the dirt or the dark at night, and truth be told, he was afraid of animals of all sizes. He bought the cottage as a symbol of his success. Stan operated a discount furniture business. He also could get you anything for wholesale.

"Just bring me a name and a number and I'll get you a good deal," he would promise.

He also would bet on anything from horseraces to football games to whether or not the sun would come up in the morning. He was a wheeler-dealer *extraordinaire*. Short and bandy legged with a sunken chest and a little pot belly, he struck a decidedly comic figure, an effect multiplied by a round, flat moon of a face, split in half by a wide smile that showed two rows of neat small teeth. He parted his jet black hair from just above his left ear and over the tops of his head in oiled strands, a futile attempt to conceal his baldness.

His grandparents had been Ukrainian immigrants, riding the rails westward in the great land rush. Their families settled in southern Saskatchewan and set about scratching a living from the earth, battered by wind, cold drought, fires and locusts.

A boy and a girl met in a one room, board-and-batten school house that also served the immigrant community as a church. After a brief courtship, they were wed and soon the first of seven children came. Stan was the last. Life was hard, but they had enough to eat and the roof over their heads was their own.

By his late teens, however, Stan knew farm life was not for him. The backbreaking physical work was more than he was willing to handle and the poverty and hardships that he knew were not what he wished for himself. He craved excitement in his life, he wanted to have money and all the trappings that went with it. Three years earlier, his older brother Mike had left Saskatchewan and moved to Toronto. Stan decided to follow him.

According to his letters home, Mike was doing all right for himself, working rackets for a small-time bookie. He was also quite good at manipulating dice, a skill that proved profitable in the many crap games that floated around town. When Stan hit the city, Mike fixed him up, calling in a favour from someone who owed him money. Within a week, Stan was delivering furniture to various stores from a distribution warehouse. Soon he was making a few extra bucks, selling items that had somehow managed to "fall off" the back of the truck.

At about this time he also noticed that on most nights, he delivered back to the warehouse several damaged items. Often the damage was slight, almost unnoticeable, yet it could not be sold. Any items that had been damaged in transit or storage were written off by the warehouse owner. Stan offered to buy the damaged goods at below cost, cash under the table. The owner would get his write-off and Stan would get what he called "primo merchandise" at rock bottom prices. He leased a store front in an immigrant neighbourhood and was soon selling "Slightly Imperfect, Brand Name Home Furnishings at Low Discount Prices". Cash and carry. He even began getting special requests for certain items, people coming in with pictures torn from newspaper ads and catalogues. Stan would vow to fill these orders, even if he had to inflict the discount damage himself.

By the time the war started, he was buying direct from furniture manufacturers, taking their seconds and remainders off their hands for them. The people who came to his stores -by 1950, he had five- didn't care about the odd scratch or nick. "Hell," they'd say, "A little mark like that? The kids'll do worse to it by the end of the week." Stan would laugh, tell the man he could see he knew how it was, and knock off another five dollars. Business was booming and by the end of the decade, he was what some people would call rich.

Sometime in those years, though, Stan and Mike had a falling out over a gambling debt. They argued, then fought, Stan emerging with a broken nose. They had not spoken in almost eight years.

Then, one day, at the track, Stan learned from a mutual acquaintance that Mike was in a downtown hospital, his smoker's cough diagnosed as lung cancer. Stan rushed to his brother's side. The years of silence forgotten. He held his hand through treatment after unsuccessful treatment, gripping his shoulders, steadying him when the radiation made him vomit, gently patting his back as he coughed up mouthfuls of blood and tissue. Three months later, on a perfect autumn day, they sat in the lounge watching in grainy black and white as Don Larsen pitched the first perfect game in World Series history, defeating the Brooklyn Dodgers. Neither man had money on the game. As Dale Mitchell struck out looking to end the game and Yogi Berra ran to the mound and leapt into Larsen's arms, Mike passed away. Stan tucked the blanket up around his brother's neck and sat, holding his hand for a long while.

Up the hill from where the boy and the old man stood surveying the tank, Stan pulled up in a butter yellow panel truck, the sides emblazoned with the announcement "Stan the Man, Fine Furniture at Below Discount Prices." Stan's head was barely visible above the steering wheel. He tooted the horn twice and hopped out. Behind the van was a half ton utility trailer, boxed with three-quarter inch plywood. He came around behind the trailer and slapped the tailgate with the flat of his hand.

"Well, Stan the Man's here," he declared in is rapid-fire delivery. Sometimes in his hurry, Stan would mix his words or even omit some entirely in a rush to spit out the next sentence. "Let's get this road on the show," he laughed at his own joke.

"Down here, Stan," the old man called up. "C'mon down and we'll figure things out."

Stan stumbled down the hill towards them. He was wearing a powder-blue pleated shirt, short sleeved and square bottomed, untucked over burgundy hounds-tooth shorts, the hems of which flapped against his knobby knees. Black nylon dress socks bagged around his scrawny ankles. Navy canvas deck shoes with white rubber soles skittered over the loose dirt.

"Geezchrist, a guy could kill himself come down that hill."

"We were tryin' to figure out how to get this thing *up* it." The old man gestured toward the tank, reeking in it's sunlit hole. "Maybe if the boy and I could lever up the front end you could get a chain under her. We could hook up to the truck and pull her out."

Stan thought about having to crawl into the hole with the evil smelling tank, wrapping his arms around it's filthy bulk to secure the tow chain.

"Yeah, yeah, sounds like an idea. But the big job be hoistin' her up. Maybe *we* oughta do that, let the boy handle th' chain."

Beside him, the boy looked down on Stan's bald patch, then across at his grandfather. The old man was trying not to laugh. "How about it?" he said to the boy.

The boy looked down at the pit, offal still seeping out from under the tank. If he didn't do it, the old man would.

"Sure, whatever."

The boy was down in the stinking hole, wedged between the side of the pit and the tank itself, trying to feed the chain underneath. Above him the two men stood, doing little more now than leaning on their levers, the boy having blocked up one end of the tank with a couple of pieces of firewood. Thankfully, the hole which spilled the contents of the tank was at the high end.

The boy was straining now, dirt stuck to his sweaty body, his face pressed against the sun-warm tank. "If I can just get it far enough so I can get it from the other side . . .," he grunted.

"Pushin' a chain," Stan commented. "Kinda like tryin' to screw without a hard-on," he cackled.

Down in the hole, the boy had scraped the skin off of the inside of his wrist. It stung with sweat. "Oh, you're a big help, you are," he said disgustedly. He climbed out of the hole, jumped over the tank and dropped down the other side. Wedging his body as deep as he could, he wormed his arm into the small space between the tank and the ground underneath.

"Careful," cautioned the old man with genuine concern. "Easy does it."

The boy's fingers searched for the tow hook on the end of the chain. At last they found it. He slipped his index finger around the throat and drew it to him. He climbed up on top of the tank, holding the hook in his fist and brought it to where the old man stood holding the other end of the chain. Taking the hook, he securely wedged it over the links of the chain.

"Good job," the old man said, brushing dirt from the boy's shoulder. "Wanna take a break?"

The boy shook his head. The sooner this job was over, the better. "Naw, let's get it in the trailer."

They had gotten the tank up the hill by hooking the chain to the trailer hitch of the truck and advancing a few feet at a time, the distance determined by the width of the road. At the end of a run, the truck would be backed up, the chain shortened and then the tank would be pulled a few more feet up the slope. As soon as it was clear of the pit, they had flipped the tank so that the hole through which the effluence escaped would be at the top.

"No use spreadin' shit all over the hill," the old man had said. Stan paled slightly at the thought.

Once at the top, they manhandled the tank into the trailer, struggling to keep the hole topside, then hitched the trailer to the truck and climbed in, Stan driving, the old man beside him, the boy comfortable on a pile of musty furniture pads in the back.

A hundred yards down the road, the trailer hit a bump while rounding a curve. The tank shifted, bounced and stayed in the bed of the trailer. Only it had rolled completely over, the hole now on the bottom, sludge pouring into the trailer box. Ignorance indeed being bliss, the occupants bounced along, unaware of the mishap and the resulting mess that would soon confront them.

In the world in which the old man and Stan had grown up, it wasn't unusual for people to go their whole lives without ever using indoor plumbing. For those who had grown up relieving themselves through a hole cut in a piece of wood, suspended over a pit dug in the middle of their own backyard, raw sewage was not considered an environmental danger. After all, they reasoned, it was only shit. It was with this level of enlightenment that the truck, the trailer and the tank, now almost empty pulled into the public dump. Their intention was to simply roll the tank out of the trailer, get back into the truck and drive away. Instead, they climbed out to be confronted by an odour that overpowered even the smell emanating from the tons of garbage that surrounded them.

Peering into the trailer, they were confronted by the sight of grey-green sludge the consistency of lumpy porridge. This gluey execrable mess piled up in the low end of the slightly tilted trailer, confirming the old plumber's adage that shit *does* indeed flow downhill. Stan gagged.

"Well, let's unload the tank first," the old man finally said resolutely.

He and the boy unhitched the trailer and tipped it back; the tank, now empty, easily rolled out. The ooze began to slide toward the tailgate. They pushed the tank into the dump and went back to consider the problem of cleaning the trailer. Stan had watched the whole operation from a distance, a look of horrified disgust on his face as though the quivering mass might suddenly assume a life of it's own and rise from the trailer, seeking to consume every living thing in it's path.

Meanwhile, the old man and the boy were busy digging through the refuse, searching for anything that might help with the clean-up of the trailer.

"Hey! I found some old curtains," the boy yelled, gathering the mildewed draperies together.

"Great!", answered the old man, his arms full of cardboard "scrapers."

Stan meanwhile darted about doing nothing particularly useful, not wanting to get dirty and, with the remembrance that bears frequented the dump looking for an easy meal, not wanting to stray too far from the truck.

The boy and the old man, standing on either side of the trailer, began swabbing out the box. After the drapes had been used up, the boy climbed into the trailer and began scraping with the pieces of cardboard.

The old man noticed some discarded paint cans, their insides shiny with hardened enamel, on the other side of the dump.

"Stan, c'mon over here and give me a hand with these pails."

Stan reluctantly left the security of the truck and went to help. The old man handed him a couple buckets, Stan took them by their handles, holding them at arms' length.

"Do you think we should be this far from the truck?" Stan asked. "There's bears around this dump, aren't there?"

"What?" said the old man distractedly. Then he caught the worry in Stan's voice. "Yeah, sure there's bears here. Saw one over in those trees just a few minutes ago." Stan snapped his head in the direction of the woods. The old man noticed Stan's reaction and grinned. "Sounded hungry, too."

"Do you think we could get back to the truck in time? You know, in case he comes this way", Stan asked, seeking reassurance.

"Nope, not a chance." The old man picked up a couple of cans.

"You don't think we could outrun them?" Stan's voice rose slightly, irrational fear taking control.

"Don't have to outrun them," the old man said. "I just have to outrun you." He started back towards the truck, smiling. Behind him, Stan scurried to catch up, empty cans banging against his bony knees.

They backed the trailer down to the government boat launch and into the water. Once in the lake, the old man and the boy kicked off their shoes, and leaving wallets and watches on the dashboard, hopped out of the truck. Carrying an old can each, they waded out to the trailer and began sluicing out the box. Stan opted to stay in the truck. Pail after pail of lake water was thrown at the gunge until finally the trailer bed was clean. At last, they piled back into the truck and headed back to the cottage.

The boy's grandmother took one look at the two of them and ordered them back into the lake. She brought them each a bar of soap and they washed themselves clean of dirt. Standing waist-deep, they removed their filthy clothes and scrubbed them as well. Tossing their now-clean clothes onto the dock, they then swam far out into the lake, savouring the cool, cleansing water. They dove deep, feeling the temperature change as they passed through the layers of stratification. Resurfacing, they gulped fresh, untainted air. Treading water gently, they slicked back wet strands of hair.

"You did a lot of work this weekend," the old man offered as a compliment.

"Thanks." The boy was glad the old man had noticed but was also embarrassed, a typical teenager, unsure of how to accept praise.

"I mean it," the old man continued. He was usually not so open with his feelings, but now he felt the need to express them to the boy. He went on, awkwardly. "That was a man's work you did, so it was."

The boy blushed with pride.

"I figure you outworked most of us . . ."

"Except Donald," the boy interjected.

"Yeah, except Donald," the old man laughed. "Anyway, I appreciate it."

"No problem," said the boy, imbuing the usually off-hand remark with a great deal of gratitude. He himself had felt for the first time that he was an equal to the rest of the men. Until now, he had "helped out," cleaning the job site, straightening nails, fetching tools. Gofer work: gofer this, gofer that. But this past weekend, he had worked beside the men, doing the same job, working with pick, shovel and axe. He had been privy to the talk of hard-working men. Joining in the laughter at crude remarks about each other's short coming, be it physical, mental or sexual, the men comfortable with his presence. It had been another rite of passage.

He didn't care that it happened over a hole in the ground and a leaky septic tank.

They began swimming back in now, slowly and lazily, alternately floating and side-stroking, blowing mists of water with their lips.

The old man stopped, treading water again, his face serious. The boy stopped alongside him, looking at him questioningly. His grandfather stared at the shore.

"What you said in the boat the other night. About it being enough. That I was willing, that I went . . . maybe you're right. Anyway, I feel better for you having said that." A muscle in his jaw twitched.

The boy felt himself swell with pride, choking him with its power. He had made an observation on a man-sized problem and now he knew he had measured up. He smiled at his grandfather, thankful for the water droplets that wetted his cheeks.

The corner of the old man's mouth lifted in a small smile, the lines around his left eye crinkling. He nodded.

"Well, let's get in and see what your grandmother has for lunch." He kicked powerfully towards shore, moving in a fluid front crawl, the boy hurrying to keep up. Still, the old man beat him by almost three lengths. When the boy emerged from the lake, dripping and gasping for breath, the old man was already standing, ankle-deep in the water. He grinned at the boy.

"What took you?" he asked.

CHAPTER 8

The cloying smell of flowers and the dry overheated air formed an almost physical barrier as they entered the funeral home. Subdued cream and gold formal patterned wallpaper and dark-stained cherry furniture presented a sober, sombre atmosphere of respectability. The funeral director, in his black coat, burgundy waistcoat and dark grey trousers greeted them politely in a hushed voice, shaking hands lightly and softly, his dry palm rasping against theirs.

"If you would care to hang up your coats and follow me, I will show you to the parlour". He pressed his thin lips together in a sad, sympathetic smile and gestured toward the coat rack. The young man and his father took the ladies coats and hung them on wooden hangers, then added their own topcoats to the rack. The director then led them down the hallway, their footsteps silent on the plush olive green carpet. An open doorway was marked with a nameplate hanging from the jamb, the white magnetic letters spelling out his grandfather's name. They hesitated a moment, then walked through the door.

The room was long and rather narrow. Against one wall stood a gold crushed-velvet couch framed by two brocaded wingback chairs. Around the perimeter of the room had been placed bronze-coloured metal folding chairs. Drab reproductions of old oil landscapes hung in ornate gilded frames. At the far end of the room, in front of a heavy gold velvet drapery and bracketed by two pewter floorlamps topped by frosted glass shades, lay the young man's grandfather. He was laid out in a dark walnut casket lacquered to a gloss so rich that the young man felt he would have to reach wrist-deep into it in order to touch the grain of the wood. Beneath the old man's head, a pillow of pure white satin shimmered like mountain snow.

The young man's grandmother seemed drawn to the open casket, unwilling yet strangely compelled, afraid of what awaited there yet unable to resist. The young man gently took her arm, placing his other hand at the small of her back. He steadied her as she made her way to the front, allowing her to set the pace. His mother and father remained at the door, receiving last minute instructions from the doting director. The young man's wife hovered somewhere in the middle, ready to assist any of them in any way should the need arise.

A few more steps and the young man and his grandmother stood beside the casket. He looked down at the familiar face of his grandfather. Yet it wasn't really him. The face was the same, although the wryness was gone from the old man's smile. His expression was one of peace, but without the mischief that had constantly danced around his eyes. The silver hair was softly swept back from his forehead, unlike the usual hard, deliberate combing the old man had always inflicted upon it. And there was something else, too, something that took the young man a moment to put his finger on. Then he realized what it was.

The weather was gone.

The lines and creases that had marked the tanned and wind-hardened skin, the permanent squint, they were gone, erased by the heavy cosmetics that left his grandfather looking like a heavily re-touched and tinted photograph. A small orange smudge of foundation soiled his white collar. But it was his grandfather's hands disturbed him the most. He remembered the old man's hands, square palmed with thick blunt fingers and calloused in more than a dozen places. Oil and grease had always delineated the creases in a web of fine dark lines. How often had he watched as those hands tied on a fishing lure or manipulate a rope into a complex, perfect knot. Cold-reddened and chapped, they had scooped slush from ice-fishing holes and tinkered with a cantankerous snowmobile engine. He had watched them swing a hammer and guide a saw, strike a match and rasp across a stubbled jaw in amusement or concentration or wonder. These hands, as much as anything else, defined the old man: his work, his play, his character.

Those hands were now shrunken and shrivelled as though emerging from a long hot bath. Robbed of their life's blood, they lay yellowed and strangely translucent, weak and ineffectual. They had been scrubbed clean, the nails scrapped and filed and buffed. Now, they could have belonged to anyone, a mannequin even. They did not belong to his grandfather. They lay softly folded on his unmoving chest, still and fragile.

"He looks good, don't you think?". Beside him, his grandmother was speaking. "Very natural," she went on, a hint of a question in her voice, seeking the young man's agreement as reassurance that her husband did indeed look fine.

He again studied his grandfather's smoothed and powdered face and the waxy, unnatural hands, searching for some recognizable sign of whom the old man had been before death. He found none.

"Yeah," he lied to his grandmother. "He looks real good. They did a real nice job."

She smiled slightly and patted the young man's hand that gently held her forearm.

* * *

The November day was raw and windy, the sky threatening snow flurries. The trees were bare of leaves, their dark limbs bending, fighting the gusts that stormed out of the northwest. Brown, desiccated leaves skittered along the ground, piling up against the curbs and fences, driven hard against the hedges and buildings. The Chevy rocked occasionally, buffeted by the wind which was now hitting the car broadside.

Inside, on the vinyl bench seat, the boy sat looking out the window, glad of the warm air blasting from the heater at his feet. Beside him, his father was hunched over the steering wheel. He coughed dryly around the cigarette that hung pasted to his bottom lip. The menthol smell of cough drops mingled with acrid cigarette smoke. He had been complaining for two days now of chest congestion. The boy glanced over at his father, concerned by the man's pallor, the steel-blue smudges under his eyes, the sheen of sweat that filmed his forehead and upper lip in spite of the chill air.

The boy and his father were running a few errands; the hardware store, pick up some dry cleaning, gas up the car and run it through the car wash. The man coughed again, grimacing and rubbing his chest in obvious discomfort.

"You don't look so good," the boy observed.

"I don't feel so good. It's this goddamned weather. I wish it'd make up it's mind." He rolled the side window down a crack and flipped his cigarette butt out into the slipstream. He immediately lit up another. "Last week, everybody's goin' around in shirtsleeves and today it feels like the middle of January." A late Indian summer had lulled everyone with it's unseasonable warmth, making the return to early winter seem that much more cruel.

"You still gonna go tonight?" the boy asked. A party was planned that evening to celebrate the forty-fifth anniversary of the marriage of the old man's brother and his wife. The boy's parents and grandparents would be attending.

The man coughed again and popped another lozenge. "Yeah, your mom wouldn't want to miss it. It's important to her. I doubt if we'll be staying late, though." He arched his back, trying to break the tightness that gripped his chest. He took another drag off of the cigarette.

The boy's father had finally gotten a desk job at the factory a year before. Almost immediately, he began putting on weight. When he was on the assembly line, the constant physical work had countered the effects of a hearty appetite. Now that he was tied to a desk, he had added twenty-five pounds to an already stocky frame. Prolonged coffee-breaks drove his pack-a-day habit up to more than two packs a day. His new sedentary lifestyle was having a decidedly adverse effect on his health.

The old man rapped on the front door before entering. The boy met his grandparents as they came in. He looked past them into the driveway, expecting to see his parents close behind. However, they were nowhere to be seen.

"Mom and dad follow you home?" he asked.

His grandparents exchanged a quick, worried glance.

"What's the matter?" the boy asked, suspiciously. "Where are they?".

"C'mon into the kitchen," the old man said. The boy followed him, fighting down a rising panic.

They sat at the table. The boy's sister joined them.

"Your mom and dad are at the hospital," the old man told them. "It's nothing too serious. Your dad's cold just got worse and . . . and they went to see if they could maybe get something for it." As a man who had always adhered to the cowboy's strict code of honour, the old man made a lousy liar

"What's really the matter?" the boy demanded.

The old man looked to his wife. She nodded once.

"He had a heart attack," the old man said quietly.

The boy's stomach turned over, cold bile splashing into his throat. He knew it. He had known it this morning . Why didn't he insist that his father go to the hospital when he had first felt the suspicion? What if he wasn't alright? What if . . .? He set his face in a mask of calm. He could not show his fear, his worry, to his sister.

"How bad?"

"Not too bad," his grandfather answered. "They've got him settled in. Your mom's with him. The doctor said it was fairly mild, more of a warning really. In a way he was lucky it happened. It might have saved him from a more serious one later on."

"I want to go up to the hospital," he said.

"Not much point. They're gettin' him hooked up in the coronary unit and they only let one person in at a time. Your mom's already there. She said she'd phone."

The boy's sister got up and left the room. He rose and followed her to her bedroom.

"What if he dies?" She was crying, sitting on her bed with her knees drawn up under her chin. The boy sat on the edge of the mattress, his hand on her foot.

"He won't die. Papa said it was a mild one. They're taking care of him."

"But what if he had died?" Her eyes pleaded with him for an answer of reassurance.

The same question had been bouncing around the boy's head from the moment he found out about his father. *What if he had died?* the boy wondered. *Would I be mature enough, strong enough to shoulder the burdens that would fall to me?* He had thought himself mature, indeed on the very cusp on manhood, eager for the privileges and responsibilities of adulthood. Now, he was lost and scared, a little boy confronted by a monster. Only he had no one to run to, no one to protect him and reassure him that everything would be alright. In fact, his sister was now looking to him for that security, that promise of life as usual.

He patted her foot. "But he didn't die," he smiled. "Try to get some sleep okay."

Still curled up, she shifted to lay on her side. He sat beside her until her breathing evened out. He was nodding himself when he heard the phone in the kitchen ringing. Covering his sister with her bed spread, he shut off her light and went out.

His grandfather was just hanging up the phone. "Your dad's doing fine. He's resting easy now. They don't think he's in any danger. I'm going up to the hospital to pick your mom up. Why don't you stay here and have a cup of tea with your grandmother. When I get back, we'll go over and get your dad's car."

The boy nodded and the old man picked up his coat and put it on. Digging in his pocket for his car keys, he went out.

The boy crossed to the stove and put the kettle on to boil. On the counter lay two packs of Player's cigarettes, their cellophane wrappers still intact. The fear and confusion the boy had felt suddenly fused into anger. The cigarettes became the enemy, the cause of his father's illness. Picking up the packs, he slowly squeezed, crushing them to death. He dropped them in the garbage.

His grandfather had picked up his mother and delivered her home. She now sat within the protective company of her mother, tiredly sipping tea at the kitchen table while her father and her son went off together to recover the car left abandoned at the party.

They drove in silence, the streetlights overhead shining down, illuminating their still faces then flashing past, plunging the interior into darkness until the next light washed over them. In their pale yellow glow the old man surreptitiously studied his grandson's face out of the corner of his eye. He was more concerned about the boy than anyone. He knew his son-in-law would recover. His granddaughter was young enough that the adults around her would protect her. His daughter would be strong and he would be there for her. But the boy. He knew how he had been raised, influenced by his father and, indeed by the old man as well. A man hid his feelings, locked his emotions deep inside. He must remain strong, a sturdy shoulder for the women to lean on. *What a crock*, the old man thought. The women in his life were twice as capable of stoicism as any man.

But in a man's world, compliments were doled out sparingly and usually tempered with a good-natured insult. A man seldom opened up to another his insecurities, fears or self-perceived weaknesses. Expressions of love were never declared, only implied through rough gestures and comments, carefully delivered to veil their true meaning from others. Macho bullshit.

The old man knew the pressure that had suddenly been dropped on the boy's young shoulders. He knew how he was struggling: the burgeoning young man fighting with the small boy. His glance now registered the set of the young jaw, the determination about the eyes. He knew the battle was raging, but that the man inside was winning, the small boy driven into submission. He only hoped that the price of victory would not be too steep.

They pulled into the parking lot of the hall where the party had been. The Chevy sat alone in the dark parking lot. Overhead, the cutting wind stampeded dark clouds across the sky, their edges silvered by the moon that peeked through every now and again. The old man pulled up beside the car and shifted into park.

"You okay?" he asked. "To drive, I mean."

"Yeah . . . fine," the boy unbuckled his seat belt, but made no move to get out. He sat staring at the dashboard.

"He's okay, you know," the old man said.

"Yeah, I know. It's just . . . I don't know. It's the thought of what . . . I don't know," he knew. He just couldn't find the words, or say them.

The old man reached across and rapped the boy's thigh twice with his knuckles. "You're doing okay." What he meant was, *I'm proud of the way you're handling this.* The boy wasn't the only one in the car having trouble saying what he meant.

"We'd better get back before the women get worried," he said.

"Yeah, I guess so." The boy reached for the door latch. He paused with his hand on it. "Papa . . . thanks." He opened the door and got out, then climbed into the Chevy, started it, and with a small wave pulled away.

The old man looked after him, a small smile crooked one side of his mouth. "You're welcome," he said softly. What he meant was, *I love you too.*

The boy's father was lying propped up in his hospital bed. His wife and daughter had already been in to see him and now he was waiting for his son. He had been in the hospital for almost a week and was, by all accounts, coming along quite well. The boy had been in to see him every day. The talk between the two had been small, questions traded back and forth about school and hospital food, part-time jobs, the weather. The answers were abbreviated as well; one word, one sentence, no more. Both were afraid to open up even slightly for fear that the floodgates would burst open and leave them embarrassed. When the fifteen minute visitation limit expired, they both suffered guilty relief.

The man lay now, mustering his strength for the visit. He had realized that morning that he had been only a year or so older than his son when he had lost his own father. This led him to thinking that thirty-nine was awfully bloody young to have had a heart attack. If his father-in-law hadn't insisted on driving him to the hospital, he might have died. He thought of all the things in his life that his father had missed. He wanted to see his children finish school and get jobs. He wanted to see them fall in love. He wanted to dance at their weddings and toast their happiness. And he wanted to know his grandchildren, to play with them and dangle them on his knee. He wanted to tell them what he knew and what life had taught him since his own children were small. He resolved to do better, to change his habits, to live to see his dreams realized. Thirty-nine was too young to die.

The boy paused in the hallway and looked through the glass wall of his father's cubicle. After four days, he thought he should be used to seeing his father like this, but each time his heart sunk into his stomach. He couldn't get over how small his father looked, pale and weak. Already, he had lost weight, which although to the betterment of his health, made him appear wasted and sickly. A dark stubble of beard only heightened the impression. Patches of his thick chest hair had been shaved in order to accept the adhesive circles that attached electrodes to his body. Wires from these sensors snaked away to monitors that beeped and flashed, graphically displaying his father's functions. A green transparent oxygen tube was strapped in place under his nose and an intravenous line dripped medication and nourishment into his body through a hypodermic shunt taped securely into the back of his right hand. The insides of both arms were bruised maroon-purple and yellow-green from the dozen or so needle sticks he had endured over the past few days. He took a deep, steadying breath and entered the room.

"Hey, Dad", he said, a contrived brightness in his voice fighting off his fear. "How are you doing?"

"Good, good," his father answered. "They figure I'll be able to transfer to a regular room tomorrow or Friday."

"Great, It'll be good to get away from all these machines, eh?"

"I don't know, when I cross my feet, I can pick up FM."

They laughed lightly at the small joke.

"You look tired." The boy's father had noticed the dark circles under his son's eyes. The slump of his shoulders. "Are you alright?"

"Yeah, I'm fine. It's just that I've got exams comin' soon and the job's gettin' busy." He had been working after school in a shoe store, four nights a week and eight hours on Saturdays. After he finished his homework and studies, it was often almost midnight before he got to sleep. Added to this already full schedule were the events of the past week. He was definitely dragging his ass.

"Your mom says you've been a big help."

The boy shrugged. "There hasn't been all that much to do."

"Still, it's good to know you're taking care of things. I appreciate it." They lapsed into an uneasy silence.

The boy finally spoke. "Well, I should get going. I've gotta go home and change before I go to work. You take care, okay. I'll be back up to see you tomorrow." Then, he reached out and squeezed his father's wrist. It was the closest thing to a hug that they had shared in a long, long time. Before he could react to it, the boy was moving out the door, tossing back a wave and a "See ya' later." The man stared after him. A tear slid down the side of his face into his side burn. He tightly closed his eyes against the burning sting. He reached one hand across his body, taking care not to disturb the I.V. line and caressed the spot where his son had gripped him. He would be able to feel the boy's touch for hours, until sleep at last overtook him.

When the boy was small, his father had loved to kiss his soft round cheeks and hold him to his chest, swaying his son to sleep. He would drink deeply the sweet baby smell, like rich warm buttermilk. He thrilled when the child would grip his finger, squeezing it in a small, fat fist, occasionally gnawing on it with hard, smooth toothless gums.

As his son grew older, changing almost overnight from an infant to a little boy, his father snatched the odd hug from the squirming little bundle of energy, looking forward to bedtime when the boy would settle down long enough to squeeze him around the neck and peck him wetly in the general vicinity of his lips. He never felt more powerful, nor, at the same time, more helpless, than when his son would come to him for comfort and protection from the fears that haunt a small boy's imagination. Sometimes, the boy would climb into the man's lap and lay his head on the man's shoulder. He would sit like that for a long time, peaceful and warm, safe and secure while his father's chest overflowed with love.

Soon, much too soon, the boy grew too big for goodnight hugs and kisses, for comforting and holding. "Baby stuff," the boy had scoffed. And it was. But neither the boy nor his father had been able to find a replacement, a new way to show affection. They fell out of practice, not sure of themselves or each other, the boy looking to his father, the man without any experience to draw upon. His own father had never hugged or kissed him, never held him to shield him from the boogie man. It left him with no idea of how to approach his own son.

It was no wonder then, that he had been so emotionally overcome by the boy's seemingly small gesture. A simple touch, a squeeze of his son's hand on his wrist had opened the door. Yet to reciprocate would have led to the man breaking down. In his experience, tears had always been a sign of weakness, or vulnerability.

His own parents had used words as weapons, verbal two-handed spear thrusts that tore into his feelings, attacking until he cried surrender. He soon learned to cover his wounds with emotional scar tissue, learned not to cry. He even learned how to attack, striking first at any perceived threat, hurting before being hurt. The only person able to occasionally break through his armour was his wife. Only she had ever seen him cry as an adult. And only a very few times.

He had never let his son see him cry, a fact which had led the boy to see tears as unmasculine. The boy had, however, not constructed a barrier from which to launch counter- or pre-emptive strikes as his father had. Instead, when threatened, he retreated further and further into himself, opting to flee rather than fight. Thus, he could withstand any assault on his emotions by withdrawing behind layer after layer of numbness.

The sight of his father so fragile, attempting to express his gratitude had caught the boy off guard. Instinctively, he had reacted, his response suppressed deep within before it could find voice. But his hand . . . his hand reached out, controlled by some long-repressed memory of the comfort afforded by physical expression.

His touch had lifted a corner of scar tissue, exposing the man's emotions, as tender and raw as the new skin under a blister.

When he awoke, the man felt a peace he had not known for a long time, not since he used to hold an infant boy to his chest, swaying gently, breathing in the baby's sweet scent, like warm buttermilk.

CHAPTER 9

The first mourners began arriving shortly after two o'clock. They gathered in the corridor, six of them, "friends of the deceased," speaking in hushed tones; small talk and nervous laughter. Dressed in their best, the men shaven and suited, the women coiffed and bejewelled, though their clothes did not give them the courage to be the first to enter, to console the grieving family.

Finally, a lone figure limped down the hall, tall, thin and stooped, his bald head uncovered. Ed Miller wore a shapeless, blue polyester suit, smelling strongly of camphor, that hung over a plaid shirt that was buttoned to the very top. He was tieless and beltless, the pants held up by grey-striped elastic suspenders. His cuffs were tucked into black zippered galoshes that softly clumped on the thick carpet. He had come by himself, having lost Marion to cancer two years before.

He stepped through the doorway and stopped to sign the visitation book, the signature large and childlike and deliberate. He laid the pen down on the book, and pulled himself erect, squaring his shoulders and his jaw. Turning, he walked across the room. The young man's father met him halfway, shook his hand, and escorted him to the widow. Ed took her hand in both of his and held it, pondering it with rheumy, red-rimmed eyes.

"I can't hardly believe it. It's a hell of a thing . . . a hell of a thing," he said.

"Thank you for coming, Ed. He always thought a lot of you, you know."

Ed nodded, thinking of what he wanted to say. For a moment, his lips moved silently, as though he hoped that by opening his mouth the right words would somehow materialize. Finally, they did.

"He . . . he was my best friend. I never told him that. I know he had lots of friends. But he was my best friend." He stopped talking, nodded a few more times, patted her hand and went to pay his respects directly to the old man. He moved quite close to the casket and then reached in and placed his hand on the old man's shoulder. He left it there for a few moments, staring at his friend's dead face, as though he could channel his thoughts and feelings down his arm and into the body, hoping it still had enough connection to the old man's soul for his message to be understood. Finally, he removed his hand and let it hang by his side.

The young man moved to his side. "Ed?"

Ed didn't look around, but acknowledged his presence by speaking.

"He was one of the good ones, you know."

"I know."

"One of the best." He raised his hand again. The young man thought for a moment he was going to place it again on his grandfather. Instead, he let it hover in the air, as though delivering a silent benediction. He turned and walked away.

* * *

They had been working for about an hour when the old man decided a break was in order. He sat down on the roof of Ed's cottage. The boy made one more trip up the ladder, carrying three bottles of beer. They were a lot lighter than the bundles of shingles he had been humping to the roof since they began this morning.

The first few loads had been the most difficult. The boy wasn't crazy about heights in the first place. Climbing up a bouncing extension ladder with a fifty-pound load balanced on one shoulder only added to his fear. The most difficult part was at the top, dismounting from the ladder onto the roof. The precarious balancing act of stepping over the top rung of the ladder onto the steeply pitched roof took all the self-persuasion the boy could muster. After all, to back down or refuse would be to appear weak.

The first trip to the roof, he had hesitated at the top, his eyes rivetted on his white knuckles locked around the ladder. He swallowed hard and tightened his abdominal muscles, trying to corral the butterflies that galloped about his stomach. Looking up he experienced the disorienting sensation created when one's entire visual frame of reference consists of nothing by sky.

Ed and the old man had been busy replacing a few rotted roof boards, but now they were looking at him expectantly.

Fighting the urge to look down, the boy gripped his load and stepped out into space. He was almost surprised when his foot hit solid wood. He was not falling. He would not die. He hadn't shit himself. He dropped the bundle and carefully made his way back down the ladder, at the bottom resisting a desire to fall to his knees and kiss the ground.

His confidence built steadily with each successive trip. By the end of the first hour, he had transferred eighteen bundles up the ladder, spreading them around the four-sided roof strategically so that when the nailers finished one pack, another would be close at hand. He moved quickly up the roof on the sides of his feet, crossing one over the other to avoid slipping on the bare wood. He came down spraddle-legged, his knees slightly bent, his toes pointing out. He learned to time the bounce of the ladder, using its springing motion to his advantage.

They sat now on the peak of the roof, cold bottles of 50 in hand, watching the lake come to life. The late June morning was warming up, the sun already climbing high in the deep blue sky. Out on the water, speedboats pulling skiers were replacing the early morning fishermen. Down the far shore, chugging for home, was a familiar sight. A fifteen-foot cedar strip fishing boat, it's upper surfaces glowing like deep amber honey, the bottom painted dark forest green, was being pushed along by a cowl-less outboard of uncertain make or vintage. Each morning at dawn the boat would motor eastward, returning a couple of hours later, the tip of a fishing rod nodding above the gunwales. The single occupant was a white-haired man, tall and lean. He straddled the rear bench, one hand on the motor's tiller, the other hand at rest upon his knee. His profile was handsome, a hawklike nose cutting the wind, the strong jaw jutting defiantly at the world. The man's name was Austin.

When the boy's sister was quite young, she had an imaginary friend she named, for some unknown reason, Patty Sue Sue. One day, while watching as Austin putt-putted up the lake, she decided that he was Patty Sue Sue's grandfather. From then on, Austin was no longer Austin to the boy's family.

"There goes Patty Sue Sue's grandpa," the old man now observed.

Ed looked out at the passing boat. "There's a strange old sonofabitch," he declared. "Never waves, never nods, never speaks."

They watched the boat labour around the point.

"Been here a long time," the old man said. "One of the first people on the lake, from what I hear. Came here some time in the twenties. The guy must be near eighty or so. Used to be an architect or something, so I hear."

"He's a strange bird," Ed repeated. "That's all I know. A strange old bird."

Austin had been born the same day as the new century, the son of a wealthy, God-fearing businessman who had made his fortune from shrewd investments, mostly in mining. Each day scores of labourers, some no more than children, would go deep underground to work twelve to sixteen hour shifts in suffocating conditions, breathing rock dust and poisonous air in exchange for subsistence wages. Occasionally, cave-ins or explosions would claim the lives of these sad creatures. Whenever he was reminded of these conditions or deaths, Austin's father would slowly shake his heavy-jowled head and mutter about "the cost of doing business."

His father was also a community-minded crusader, leading campaigns to rid their city of evil, targeting such subversives as prostitutes and beggars, homosexuals and immigrants, Catholics and Jews. For this dedication and hard work, he received numerous awards and honours from society's more-esteemed organizations.

As soon as he was old enough, Austin was sent away to one of the country's oldest and most respected boarding schools. It was there he discovered a love of architecture and drafting. He would spend hours in the library, pouring over diagrams of the great cathedrals, becoming in particular a disciple of Christopher Wren. At a very early age, he had found his calling, his life's passion.

It was at boarding school, too, that he discovered his attraction to other males. At first it was merely experimentation, you show me yours and I'll show you mine. At sixteen, however, he was shocked to discover that he had fallen in love with a male classmate. He was deeply disturbed by this realization, having been raised to believe that these deviant desires were terrible, sinful feelings that would condemn him to hell, to eternal damnation. Despair plunged him into a severe depression. He lost weight, experienced terrible headaches and stomach pains. He even contemplated suicide.

His father was so concerned by his son's condition, that he immediately sent Austin north to a wilderness summer camp, believing that the fresh air and warm sunshine would cure the troubled lad.

It was here that Austin fell in love again, only this time it was with the land. The clear, deep lakes and dark verdant forests rejuvenated him. The clean, pine-scented air and the still peacefulness calmed his soul. He knew, then, that his father's god, vengeful and stringent, condemning and wrathful, was not capable of creating this world. The God that created all this was a God of forgiveness, a God of beauty and love, a God of happiness and peace and contentment. The revelation transformed Austin. No longer would he wither in self- recrimination. He would spread his discovery of God through his architecture. He would not build churches that would be dark, subdued prisons of fear and self-loathing, where people entered with eyes downcast with shame and unworthiness. Instead, Austin vowed to create towers of light and air where people would gather in peace and joy, raising their eyes to the heavens and embrace God with all their hearts, thanking him for his unconditional love and acceptance. He would build homes, and workplaces for these people, releasing them from the dark, dreary formality and the soul-killing drudgery in which they now existed. Austin had never felt so free.

Upon returning to school, he launched himself into his studies. Soon he was far ahead of the other students. At nineteen, he was in his final year of university. Every summer, he found a way to return north.

One day in the spring of his final year, it happened again. Austin fell in love, this time with a gentle young man only a year older than himself. They met while playing tennis and soon they developed a fast friendship. When tentative advances were not rebuffed, they knew. Friendship led to affection. Affection led to love. They began spending as much time together as possible, though careful to avoid any public display of their true feelings.

One evening however, as they walked across the campus grounds, they felt safe, cloaked by the darkness, the park empty of people. They joined hands, feeling the thrill that all young lovers do when strolling hand in hand beneath an early summer's moon. They were oblivious to the rest of the world.

Perhaps that is why they didn't notice the group of young thugs who had been prowling the grounds, looking for any kind of trouble they could get into. Two young men holding hands, was more than they could have hoped for. From behind, they rushed the two, knocking them to the ground. Shouting and cursing, they began beating the two young men. After a few minutes, the unfortunate couple were jerked to their feet, the metallic taste of blood in their mouths, it's sweet odour hanging in the air. Austin breathed painfully behind broken ribs. The thugs held them tightly from behind as the ringleader stepped before them and spread his arms.

"Brothers and sisters," he intoned in an imitation of a fire and brimstone preacher, "what we have before us here is a couple of sinners. Now, as you all know, the Lord sayeth that a dog must not lay down with a cat and a pig must not layeth with a sheep." He was grinning malevolently now. "And a man *must* not layeth with another man." He punctuated his point by kneeing Austin in the groin. His friend struggled to help him, but screamed as his shoulder was wrenched from it's socket. "It is thus, that we have been sent to deliver the wrath of God."

With the pronouncement, the two young men were again knocked to the ground. Austin immediately curled, his knees protecting his belly, his arms covering his head. Furious kicks thudded against his body, searching for any chink in his defences. None, however, got through to inflict any serious damage.

His friend was not so fortunate. With is damaged arm now dangling uselessly at his side, he was not able to afford himself the protection that Austin had. Hard boots battered his body, cracking his ribs and damaging organs. A lung was punctured and collapsed. His nose and jaw were broken, his cheekbone crushed. He began to vomit. A final brutal kick caught him in the right temple, splinters of bone driving deep into his brain. He didn't feel the rest of the beating.

When the thugs finally broke off their attack and fled into the night, Austin crawled to his lover. He found him still and lifeless.

The newspaper publisher was a crony of Austin's father, responsible for reporting the good deeds of the man and nominating him for most of his honours. Out of respect for his old friend, he suppressed the story. He did, however, inform Austin's father of the details of the attack. All the details.

Austin's father was outraged, not at the beating and thuggery, but at the fact that his own son was a homosexual, a sodomite. He went to see Austin in the hospital. He gave him a cheque for ten thousand dollars, his "inheritance" he called it, and told Austin he wanted nothing more to do with him.

Austin took the money and obeyed his father's wishes. Retreating to his beloved north, he bought a lot on the edge of the lake and designed and built a small cottage, filling it with light and air.

Five years later his father died of complications from syphilis, a condition he caught from one of the many prostitutes he habitually frequented. The coroner was a friend. He listed the cause of death as "natural causes."

Austin stayed away from the funeral. Instead he made the daylong drive to his cottage. Standing on the rocky shoreline, he raised his eyes to the sky and asked God to have pity on his father's soul.

The boat was now out of sight, the sputter of its motor fading in the distance. They watched as its wake sloshed on the far shore.

"He is an odd one. Lives up here year 'round now, all by himself. Has a nice place, though," Ed said. "Lots of windows."

The old man sat for a minute. "He's always alone," he commented. "His wife must be dead or something." Clambering to his feet, he brushed off the seat of his pants. "Well, I s'pose we oughtta get back to work."

Ed and the boy rose to follow him back up the ladder.

They had been at the roof for a little over five hours now and had already taken four breaks. The boy had worked through the last one, carrying up the last of the bundles. He then began fastening shingles, working two rows at a time. The old man called another break.

"Let's take a breather, guys. Who's goin' for the drinks?"

"Dumb question," the boy muttered as he headed for the ladder. He shinnied down and went into the kitchen.

"Another break? Already?" his grandmother asked. She and Marion were at the kitchen counter, making lunch. This morning's bacon was being reheated in the oven and Marion was slicing a tomato just picked from the vines she grew in the sunroom window. His grandmother was buttering toast. The delicious odour set the boy's stomach to rumbling. He hadn't realized how hungry he was. Now, he was suddenly ravenous.

"Yeah, it seems we spend more time takin' breaks than we do working," he said. He grabbed three bottles of beer from the fridge and snapped the caps. He turned to leave.

"Well, they're gettin' old," said Marion. "I know Ed doesn't have the stamina he used to." She nudged the boy's grandmother. The two women dissolved into giggles then immediately began shushing each other, nodding towards the boy.

He knew what they meant, but pretended not to notice. It was ridiculous. His grandparents? Ed and Marion? He got a mental picture of Ed, but immediately pushed it from his mind before he laughed. Maybe when they were young they did it. But not now, God, no. Not at their age. I mean, all those wrinkles and no teeth and stuff. The boy opened the door with his elbow.

"Tell them lunch will be ready in a few minutes, okay," Marion said. The woman had managed to compose themselves.

"Okay," he said and went out, the door slamming behind him. He heard a murmur of a voice from the kitchen, he could not make out which woman it was. Whoever it was and whatever they said elicited another flurry of giggles. The boy rolled his eyes. *Maybe they're not too old,* he thought and shrugged.

They had finished lunch and now sat in the shade of the Millers' cottage, finishing their drinks.

The old man sighed. "Well, I guess we should get started," he said although he made no move to get up.

Beside him, Ed belched and scratched his stomach. "Yeah, I guess so," he said resignedly. "Gotta go see a man about a lizard first, though." He pushed himself out of the lawnchair.

Beside the boy, the old man's head started to nod, his eyelids weighted with sleep. His breathing grew deep and slow and his mouth hung slack. Less than a minute after deciding that they should return to work the old man began to snore.

The boy took the opportunity to study the old man. He was startled to find that, although the man next to him was his grandfather, he didn't quite recognize him. The steel grey hair had turned silvery white and the pink patches of scalp, once vainly disguised, had grown too large to successfully hide. His face, still tanned and wind-toughened, had gained a degree of softness, like old leather worn thin and supple. Its wrinkles, once hard and taut, now had begun to sag and droop, forming jowls and cheek pouches and bags beneath his eyes. A wattle had formed under his double chin, connecting his head to a crepe chest. Clumps of hair grew unchecked from his ears. Here and there from the bushy white eyebrows, dark wiry hairs sprung out rebelliously. His cheeks were coloured not only by the sun, but also by fine webs of burst blood vessels. The old man remained a stranger for only a moment, then the veil lifted and the boy once again recognized the familiar face of his grandfather. Still, the moment left him feeling unsettled. It was not until later that afternoon that it would come to him. His grandfather was getting old. Not older. Old.

The old man was nearly sixty. People died at sixty. The boy was taken aback by this sense of mortality. He began to wonder how much longer he would have his grandfather with him. They were just now becoming more than a grandfather and grandson. They were friends, adult friends. They talked now of many things, sharing experiences, entertaining one another, seeking advice and opinions. The boy felt a stab of fear. How much longer until he lost this friend.

The boy was not the only one experiencing a new look at a familiar face that day. Earlier, while sitting with Ed on the roof, the old man had watched the boy work through the break, carrying the last of the shingles up to the roof.

"Not afraid of hard work, is he?" Ed said.

"No, but he was sure afraid of that ladder." They chuckled at the memory of the boy's first few trips to the roof, his eyes wide, showing white all around, his lips tightly pressed together lest he cry out, betraying his fear.

"He got over it, though," said Ed. "Look at him."

The boy was just now coming to the top of the ladder, another bundle on his shoulders. He moved from the ladder to the roof in one easy motion, not even breaking stride. He moved up the roof and dropped the shingles. He turned to the two men.

"Two more bundles to go," he said grinning, "then break time's over." He returned to the ladder, flashing another grin before he descended from view.

"Look at him." Ed's words rolled around in the old man's brain. For a moment, the boy that stood in front of him was six years old, a black felt cowboy hat above a smile that showed a brand-new space. The little boy quickly disappeared and in his place was a young man, hands on his hips. He was a shade under six feet tall, long-legged and slim-hipped. His denim work shirt was unbuttoned and untucked revealing the beginnings of dark curly hair that dusted his chest and stomach. Faded Levi's were rumpled into the top of battered Kodiaks. A mass of dark brown hair boiled out from under a black baseball cap and fell to the young man's shoulders and a soft stubble shadowed his jawline. Then he grinned and the boy leapt from his brown eyes and crooked smile and the old man felt his uneasiness leave him. He shouldn't really be surprised, though. After all, the boy had been showing a definite maturity in the last year or so. His observations and opinions were no longer the impulsive outbursts of youth, but had become considered and thoughtful. The boy disagreed more with the old man and his father, no longer accepting their ideas as absolute. He would argue his case, sometimes conceding their point, other times disarming them with surprising logic. Still, if he thought he was right, he would stick to his guns, although with a diplomacy that deferred to the boy's elders and left no wounded feelings. He had his mother's sensitivity and quiet strength and his father's sense of justice and his biting, sometimes dark humour. He also had the old man's sense of mischief and habit of daydreaming.

The old man looked as Ed had commanded. He was happy with what he saw.

They worked from lunch until dinner with only one break, that coming because of pain and laughter. Ed's pain. Everybody else's laughter.

The boy and old man were working their way across one side of the roof while Ed worked away opposite them. They knew Ed had an accident when they heard him.

"Ow, doddan thono'bitth."

They scurried to the peak of the roof and looked over. Ed was doing a small dance of pain, his thumb in his mouth.

"What happened, Ed?" the boy asked.

"I hid by thum wid duh doddan hanber."

They looked at one another, nostrils flaring to keep from laughing. The old man turned back to Ed.

"Ed, take your thumb out of your mouth so we can understand you. Now again, what happened?"

Ed jerked his thumb from his mouth. "Ya dozy bastards. I said I hit my goddamned thumb with the goddamned hammer." He plunged his throbbing thumb back into his mouth.

"You're not supposed to hammer your thumbnail, Ed, just the roofing nails," the old man teased.

"Wery fuddy," Ed aimed a kick at the hammer lying on the roof. The shingle he was standing on was not yet nailed down and it skidded under his foot. He fell and rolled down the roof and over the eaves.

Worried now, the boy and the old man hurried down the ladder to discover Ed tangled in the large juniper bush that had broken his fall. He struggled, apparently unhurt, trying to find purchase to help himself up. He flailed away, cursing a blue streak. Relieved to find nothing more serious than a few scratches, they each took an arm and helped Ed to his feet.

The old man ran a concerned eye over him and found damage only to Ed's pride. "C'mon Ed," he said. "Quite screwing around, we got work to do."

Marion came rushing out of the cottage just then. "My God, Ed, what happened? Are you all right? What happened?" she asked.

"I hit my goddamned thumb and fell off the goddamned roof," he examined a skinned elbow. "I'm all right."

"What did you do that for?" she asked.

"I thought it'd be fun, fer crissakes," he sneered. "Don't ask stupid questions, woman."

"Let's take a break," the old man suggested. He put his hand on Ed's shoulder. "Thought we'd lost you old buddy."

For the next twenty minutes, they enjoyed cold drinks and imitations of Ed falling off the roof. The women howled with laughter, spurring the old man on to more exaggerated flailing. Soon, even Ed joined in.

The boy's grandmother came out of the cottage.

"Boys," she called up to them. "Come on down and get cleaned up. Supper's almost ready."

Considering all the breaks, they had done a good day's work. They would easily finish the next day. Only a few more rows of shingles and the caps remained to be put in place. They collected the tools and descended the ladder. The steaks were almost done. A bowl of potatoes, roasted with slices of onion and carrots, kept warm beneath a tinfoil cover.

The men washed and then seated themselves at Ed and Marion's kitchen table. They passed around the potatoes, then the grilled steaks. They ate quietly, tired from the work and the fresh air. Outside, the sun was an orange-pink ball slipping down in a blue-grey sky. As it neared the horizon, it turned the skyline red.

"Red sky at night, sailors' delight," said the old man.

Ed nodded. "Good day to work tomorrow."

Across the lake, a cedar strip boat putted along the shore, it's wake two black folds edged with silver.

"There goes Patty Sue Sue's grandpa, out for his evening fish," the old man said.

His grandmother looked out the window wondering if he was a widower. She considered the possibility, saddened that it could be true. For Austin. For all of them.

CHAPTER 10

The visitation would last only one day, from two until four thirty in the afternoon, and again that evening from six until nine. The service would be held the following morning. It was now just past three and the young man's mother and grandmother sat on the gold velvet couch. Flanking them, sitting on folding chairs, were his sister and her boyfriend. The young man and his father kept busy ushering visitors around the room. The young man's wife moved quietly about the room, seeing that everyone was taken care of. She had a way of always being exactly where she was needed. The young man caught her eye and winked. She smiled back. A wink was their secret sign meaning "I love you." They winked at each other often.

After Ed had left, the mourners came in steadily, sometimes in pairs, others in bunches. In the early afternoon, most of the visitors were elderly, retirees who had not other daytime obligations. They shuffled in, hesitant, almost fearful. They visited this place frequently now as they grew older, their friends dying off, taking with them a piece of familiar ground, leaving those who remained more and more alone. They feared that they might be the next to die, but fearing, too, that they might be the last.

Some of the mourners didn't know what to say, stumbling over their words, only their eyes and handshakes eloquently expressing their grief. Others went on and on, believing their words to be a comfort when, in fact, the widow wished they would just shut up. After a couple of minutes, one of the family would interrupt with another introduction or a question ("Excuse me, but have you met . . .", "I'm sorry to butt in, but do you know where

. . ."). These distractions usually allowed the widow to escape these well-wishers.

Stan came that afternoon, dapper in a custom tailored navy pinstripe wool suit. A diamond pinky ring flashed in the pale light, as his hands worried the brim of a dove grey fedora. He stood before the casket, his lips quivering. He wiped at his eyes, pushing his glasses up on his forehead. The young man stood behind him. Stan turned and shook his hand, forcing a small smile.

"Thank you for coming, Stan," he said. Stan nodded back and went to speak to the young man's grandmother.

"I'm very sorry, very sorry," he said. "Are you all right? Can I do anything? Anything at all?"

He stepped closer and took her elbow, turning her away from the others, he lowered his voice and spoke into her ear. "Are you okay . . . financially? Money-wise, I mean." His right hand slipped inside his jacket, reaching for his billfold.

She smiled, a real smile, one of the very few smiles that day, touched by his offer. Crass though it appeared, she knew that money was the god to which Stan prayed. What he had offered was more than a few dollars. His wallet was his soul and he had been ready to reach in and give her a piece of it. She gripped his arm and kissed him on the cheek. "Thank you Stan, but I'm fine."

Stan blushed and cleared his throat. "Well, okay . . . good . . . good. If you ever need anything, you just give me a call, you hear."

The young man interrupted. "Good to hear that Stan. We have a septic tank to move this weekend."

Stan blinked behind thick bifocals for a moment, trying to place the reference. Then he remembered and a smile creased his face. He reached into his pants pocket and tossed the young man a quarter.

"Hire someone," he growled.

While the young man and his grandmother were talking with Stan, a woman entered, her dyed-orange hair tucked under a stylish green-felt hat. Tears smudged her mascara and left a dark track down her heavily powdered cheek. Alex's wife approached the coffin. She had lost Alex six years earlier, an aneurysm taking him in his sleep. Everyone thought she would be helpless without his constant pampering. She surprised them by buying a condo, learning to drive and joining a local theatre troupe. Right now, she was rehearsing for her starring role as *Auntie Mame.*

She escorted herself to the casket. As she looked down at the old man, she felt her heart breaking, the same as it had broken when Alex had died. It was her secret that she had always carried something of a torch for her brother-in-law. She had never told anyone, not even her husband. No one.

She had first fallen for him when she was a peroxide blonde riding alongside Alex in his convertible coupe. She liked his cocky swagger and the naive innocence it did not quite disguise. The rebellious grin and the mischievous eyes had stolen her heart. Yet he was a gas jockey with no money and no future. She had grown up listening to her father preach of the terrors of poverty and had no intention of living the rest of her life that way. So she stuck with Alex. He treated her like a queen, fulfilling all of her material wishes. And, after all, sex, she knew, lasted only a few short minutes, while poverty could be forever.

She slipped her hands out from under her dark-green wool cloak and removed one soft black glove, revealing a lily white hand with manicured, coral-coloured nails. She pressed the tips of the first two fingers to her lips, then lightly touched the edge of the coffin.

"Always," she whispered.

The factory where the old man had worked before retiring five years before let out at half past three. Soon former co-workers of the old man, began filing in, stopping on their way home from work. Fellow supervisors paraded in, puffed with their own self-importance, wearing white short-sleeved dress shirts and pen-filled pocket protectors, clip-on ties and heavy black safety shoes.

The day after he retired, the old man had carefully folded his shirts and laid his three clip-ons across them, smoothing them out with the knife-edge of his hand. On top of the pile he placed his pocket protector. He gently slid it all into a paper bag and neatly rolled the top closed. He picked up a glass of rye and silently toasted the brown-papered bundle. Tossing back the shot, he collected the bag and ceremoniously dropped it down the incinerator chute. "Good riddance," he called after the falling bundle.

Others arrived, too. Men dressed in jeans and T-shirts, workboots, some in coveralls. These were the people who had worked for the old man. Once upon a time, he had been one of them. As he worked his way up into management, he kept in mind where he had come from. Then, all he had wanted was to be treated fairly, decently and with respect for a hard day's work. It was his philosophy that you did not *manage* men, you *led* them. Respect was something you earned, not something you demanded. These men came to pay their respects.

Soon, it was four-thirty and the parlour emptied out. The young man's parents were taking his grandmother out for dinner. His sister and her boyfriend were going as well.

"I'll stay here, just in case someone comes by," the young man said. "Bring me back something okay. I'll eat in the lounge."

"I should stay, too," his wife said.

"No, it's okay, you go ahead."

She was about to protest when she saw something in his eyes and she knew he wanted to be alone.

"Okay," she said. "We won't be long." She kissed him lightly on the lips. "You're sure you'll be okay?" He nodded. She smiled and winked at him. He winked back. Message received.

The young man did indeed want to be alone. He had always savoured the time spent with his grandfather, just the two of them. This would be the last opportunity he would have.

When everyone was gone, he loosened his tie and undid the top button on his shirt. He pulled a folding chair over near the casket where he would be able to see his grandfather's face. He opened his jacket, hitched his pants and sat down, leaning forward with elbows on his knees, his hands clasped in front of him. He thought about all the times they had spent like this, sitting and watching the world, sometimes talking, often times not. For them it was enough to be together, as though their thoughts telepathically travelled between them, rendering spoken words unnecessary.

The night spent sitting on the deck while the rest of the cottage slept, when they watched the Aurora Borealis chase across the sky, a dancing curtain of yellow and pink.

Camping beneath an open sky, gazing at the stars, more and more becoming visible the longer they looked, the Milky Way silver dust across black velvet. They lay staring until the universe seemed to take on dimensional shape and form, no longer infinite.

Standing on the end of the dock watching a storm sweep across the water, the sky yellow-grey, the air thick and ominous. At the far end of the lake, clouds boiled. A blast of hot wind hit them suddenly. Thunder rolled and sheet lightning flashed and a veil of rain moved steadily toward them. They stepped into the shelter of the boathouse just as a seemingly solid wall of water descended on them, reducing the opposite shore to a barely discernible shadow.

Sitting on a warm June evening on a grassy hill over-looking the Saskatchewan river, watching a spectral herd of long-dead bison race across the Prairie, Indian hunters riding their flanks, firing arrows into their midst. The cloud of dust vanished with the echoing thunder of hooves and the screams of the riders, leaving only the deepening dusk over the short new grass.

Hours spent on the water, rods and reels in hand, watching the sun rise or set, letting the peacefulness wash over them, cleansing their souls.

They had always been together, "pardners" the old man would say, vicariously riding the range with "The Virginian" and Rowdy Yates, Matt Dillon and Cheyenne Beaudie. Even when the boy had grown into his teens, they would sit into the wee hours of the morning, the cottage illuminated only by the blue glow of the television watching the Duke and Jimmy Stewart gun down Lee Marvin in "The Man Who Shot Liberty Valance" or Gary Cooper walking out alone to face almost-certain death at "High Noon".

They were two of a kind, grandfather and grandson, friends and companions. Cowboys and fishermen.

The evening visitation was much busier. A steady line formed to greet the family and view "the deceased" as the funeral director would say.

The young man was introduced to many people he did not know, friends from his grandparents' past and even some relatives he had never met before. To his amusement many of the men, most now in their fifties and sixties, still answered to childhood nicknames. By the night's end, he had met a Pinky and a Bing, a Buzzy and a Boomer, a Mush and a Hap and a Bucky, a Beaver and a Squirrel. He began to understand when he found they had been saddled with given names like Clarence and Delbert and Elmer. Still, he had to struggle to keep a straight face when introduced to a dignified, well-dressed businessman and be told "Call me Snuffy. All my friends call me Snuffy."

Most of the people continued to mill around long after paying their respects. They stood in small clusters, catching up on things, many not having seen one another since the last funeral. They would get caught up in their conversations and, forgetting where they were, someone would laugh out loud. Immediately, the laugh would turn to a cough, the culprit guilty and ashamed to have experienced a moment of happiness at such a sad occasion.

Donald lumbered in with Alex's daughter on his arm. He was well over three hundred pounds now, his collar swallowed by flesh, his tie able to reach only halfway down his mountainous shirt front. When it came time to offer his condolences, he fidgeted, afraid he would sound stupid.

"I . . . I'm sorry for your loss," he said and admonished himself for being so cliché. He hadn't said what he felt, what he had wanted to say.

He meant something to everyone here, Donald wanted to say, looking around the room. *This is the legacy your husband is leaving. All these people were touched by him, changed by him. Their children and grandchildren will be changed because these people knew him. He is leaving a piece of himself to everyone who has ever known him. He made a difference.*

Donald struggled for a way to say this. Finally, he put it simply, by saying "He mattered, you know. These people, they won't forget him." He hoped he had not made a fool of himself. To the contrary, he had spoken the most comforting words the widow had heard all day.

The dining table was illuminated by a single metal-shaded light that hung from the ceiling. In its soft pool of yellow-white, the young man sat, a mug of tea held in both hands. It was almost three o'clock in the morning. He ran a hand over his hair and took a sip from the cup. The tea was only lukewarm now. He held it behind his teeth for a moment before swallowing.

His wife came into the room, her face soft with sleep. She wore the white cotton nightshirt he had gotten for her that Christmas and her dark hair was mussed and she attempted to tame it now with her fingers.

"Can't sleep?" she asked.

"I'll be in in a little while."

She stepped behind him and began to knead his shoulders, feeling the knotted muscles under her fingers.

He groaned, first with pain, then with relief and bowed his head forward, stretching his neck and upper back, feeling the burn as she massaged away the tension that had built up over the past few days.

"Are you okay?"

"Yeah. I'm just not looking forward to tomorrow."

"I know." She moved around and took the chair beside him, leaning her elbows on the table, her chin resting in the heel of her hand. She was extremely beautiful. Not striking, maybe not what others might call a head-turner, just quietly, naturally, beautiful. A thick mass of chestnut hair framed an oval face of pale skin as smooth and flawless as porcelain. She had large butterscotch eyes, flecked with gold. Fine lines creased the corners when she was worried, like now. When her full, blush-coloured lips pulled into a smile, her eyes would light up above apple cheeks and her nose would crinkle. Even now, at three in the morning, she was beautiful.

He had met her at a party at the house of a mutual friend, noticing her the moment she walked in the door, tight blue jeans and a tighter white T-shirt. To be honest, it was what was in the T-shirt that first caught his attention.

Neither of them was seeing anyone and so when the rest of the couples retreated to the darkened family room for some serious necking, they say in the kitchen, talking. He had stopped staring at her T-shirt once he had noticed the flashing smile and teasing eyes. He did his best to make her laugh. She was beautiful when she laughed. When it was time for her to go, he walked her to her car. As they stood close in the dark, not wanting to say goodnight, he realized he had never wanted to kiss anyone as badly as he wanted to kiss this girl.

He called her the next day and arranged their first official date. They saw each other almost every day after that. On the third date, they kissed, softly. Nothing had ever been so sweet on his lips.

* * *

He brought her to the cottage that September. The first frost of autumn had yet to touch the forest, the leaves showing only the beginnings of the riotous colour they would soon display. The sun enveloped the canopy, seeming to illuminate the trees from within.

They had arrived the night before, and this morning he had kissed her awake in time for breakfast. She had smiled sleepily and stretched, the jersey nightgown tightening across her body. He kissed her again, inhaling deeply her morning scent, cinnamon and sandalwood, wild and exciting. He ran his fingers lightly across her belly.

"I'd better go," he grinned. "Breakfast in five minutes." She turned and left the room.

She stretched again, running her own fingers up her body. She wished he could have stayed.

They sat on a dome of granite overlooking the east arm of the lake, the sun-warmed rock relaxing the muscles in their legs. From this vantage point, they looked over a stand of shoreline poplars, their golden-green leaves trembling in the warm breeze. Beyond the trees, the lake reflected the high blue sky; the sun a million jewels on it's rippled surface.

She was sitting up, his head craddled in her lap. She stroked his forehead, careful to avoid the band-aid that covered the lump on his left temple.

"How's your head?" she asked, her face a concerned frown.

"Oooh," he groaned. "I guess I'll be okay. Nothing a kiss or two wouldn't cure."

She flicked him lightly on the nose with her finger. "I'll kiss you alright."

That morning, after breakfast, they had gone for a walk along the shoreline. He had reached down and picked up a flat stone and skimmed it across the water. It skipped four times as it pattered across the surface. It was something he had learned to do as a young boy, his grandfather teaching him the basics, his father perfecting his motion so that the stone not only skipped well, but so he looked good throwing it, too.

She picked up a stone of her own and threw it with all her might. *Plop.* She tried again. *Plop.*

"Hey, that's good," he teased. "You hit the water."

"Have you been told today?" she asked, feigning menace.

"Now, now. Ladies don't use language like that."

"Up yours."

He selected another stone. "Here, hold it like this." He demonstrated, the stone curled inside his index finger, steadied with his thumb. He handed her the stone.

"Like this?"

He nodded. "Okay, now." He stepped behind her, taking her throwing hand in his. He circled her waist with his other arm, feeling the soft weight of her breast on his wrist. *I hope she's a slow learner*, he thought. "It's all in the wrist. Keep your arm down below your waist. Like that." He lowered her arm to the correct position. "Now, keep your wrist out in front of the stone until you let go with your thumb, then snap the rest of your hand forward." He guided her through the motion a couple of times. "Got it?" He stepped back.

She let fly, the stone skipping once.

"Not bad, not bad," he said, handing her another stone. "Try it again. Remember to keep your arm down." He squatted and began to collect more throwing stones.

She drew her arm back and thought of all the pieces of advice he had given her. Catching her lip between her teeth in concentration, she threw. Somewhere between the windup and the release, some signals had gotten crossed. Instead of spinning out across the water on a perfect, flat trajectory, the rock flew off to the side, striking him in the head. He pitched forward onto his hands and knees. Horrified, she covered her mouth with her hands and dropped to his side. He blinked a few times then sat up on his knees and touched his forehead where blood seeped from a deep scrape. He started to laugh.

"You must still be doing something wrong," he said. "It still only skipped the once."

He had never really been comfortable around girls, shy and afraid of being rejected. The few girls he had dated, he had not gotten close to, physically or emotionally. Attempts at any sort of intimacy had been awkward and unnatural, completely unfulfilling. Yet here he was with his head nestled in the lap of this beautiful girl, entirely at ease, finding delicious contentment against her warmth, soothed by her touch.

"I love you." He said it and he meant it. He meant it with all his heart.

The finger that had idly been tracing his ear stopped moving. She couldn't have heard him right. "What?" she asked, hopefully, yet also afraid he might repeat it, at the same time afraid he might not.

"I said, I love you."

He said it and it frightened her. She braced herself for what would come next; hands at her breasts, grasping, almost clawing while she fought to protect herself, the fumbling, clumsy groping, painful between her legs. Her experience with boys had always been like that. They would say anything, do anything, promise the world to secure her trust and affection. Then when they found that she wasn't willing to go the next step, they would storm off, leaving her alone, feeling cheap and dirty even though she had allowed nothing. She had been hurt often enough to know that she never wanted to be hurt again.

Yet, there was something about *this* boy, something in the way he kissed her and touched her, tentatively and easily, naturally. When she would ask him to stop, he wouldn't persist, but would seem almost apologetic. Maybe this time, it would be all right. And she did know how she felt about him. She gathered her courage and her trust.

"I love you, too," she said softly.

He smiled and lay his head back in her lap, closing his eyes. He sighed, "So, what are you doing for the rest of your life?"

"No plans," she answered.

They took their time walking back to the cottage, holding hands, letting their bodies brush together. All around them, the forest prepared for winter. Trees and plants shed their fruit and seeds. Overhead, squirrels chattered and raced along branches, leaping from tree to tree, building up their winter stocks. Chipmunks darted amidst the understory, their cheeks bulging with food that would see them through the coming months. A blue jay, vivid cerulean against the yellow-gold of an early autumn maple, scolded their passing. The sumac was already dressed in its fall finery, a thicket of deep scarlet.

They passed the hermit's house, now collapsed, a victim of time and neglect and heavy snows. The beaver pond was now almost completely covered over by marsh grasses. In a few more years its transformation to a luxurious meadow would be complete.

As they came to the road behind the cottage, they stopped and kissed, tenderly at first, then fiercely and passionately, their bodies pressed tightly together. When they separated, they were both trembling. They smiled secret smiles at one another and stepped out into the sunlight. Hand in hand they walked down the path to the cottage door.

"And fifteen-two is twelve." She counted off the holes. "That's the game."

The old man flipped his cards on the table and sat back in his chair with a huff. She had just beaten him at cribbage for the third straight game, including one skunk. He had tried to make excuses, blaming lousy hands and bad luck, but the truth was, she was a helluva crib player.

She gathered the cards together and began tapping them into order, amused at his sour expression. "Sorry," she said.

"No you're not."

She treated him to a smile. "Want to go again?"

He thought about it. His luck had to change soon. He couldn't lose four in a row, could he? "Sure, let's go."

She handed him the cards. "Loser deals first," she smiled sweetly.

The old man and the boy stood on the deck, elbows propped on the railing. Two more straight cribbage losses had convinced the old man to call it quits. He retreated outside to escape the shame of his defeat at the hands of a woman.

The night air was cool and moist and the old man blew out a stream of breath, watching it condense into a billowing cloud. "Frost tonight, I think," he said.

Beside him, the boy said nothing. He was thinking about walking her to her room that night. She had stopped at the door and turned her face to him, her eyes searching his.

"What you said today. Do you really?"

"Do I love you?" He paused for a moment, not wanting to answer too quickly, not wanting to sound off-hand. "Yes. Yes, I really do love you." He traced the curve of her throat with his fingertip and softly kissed her lips. They finished the kiss and pulled apart, their eyes still closed. He inhaled deeply and looked at her again. "Goodnight."

"Goodnight." She turned and stepped into the bedroom.

"Hey."

"Hmm?"

"I really do love you, too."

He smiled and reached for the door-handle. "Goodnight," he said once more as the door closed between them.

It was this memory that now caused him to smile again into the darkness. The old man noticed it and knew what it meant.

"I like her," he said. Actually, he was a little bit in love with her, himself. He realized this when he was losing his fifth straight game to her and found that he didn't seem to mind. Of course, he didn't love her in the same way as his grandson , more like a daughter or maybe a granddaughter. Although he did have to admit that she was awfully good-looking, just the same.

"I like her, too." He didn't yet want to share the fact that they had declared their love for one another, wanting instead to keep it to himself, savouring the warm, full feeling it brought him.

The old man didn't need to be told. He had seen the looks that had passed between them, the way they held hands, walking unhurriedly, somehow sensing that they had the rest of their lives to get to where they were going. He had felt that way himself, once. He still felt like that sometimes.

"Not too hard on the eyes, either," he continued. "I'd have to say she's a keeper." In fishing vernacular, this was a compliment of the highest degree.

"Yeah, I think so, too."

"I wouldn't be too quick to throw her back, if I was you. Matter of fact, I don't know that I'd throw her back at all." He cast a side-long glance, searching to see the effect of his words.

The boy grinned self-consciously. He had found himself thinking along these very same lines, lately. The idea of sharing the rest of his life with this one girl confused him, yet it also excited him. Until he had met her, his experience with the opposite sex had been the adolescent fumblings of teenage infatuation fueled by raging hormones and curiosity. With this girl, though, it was different. He was aroused by the way she reacted when he caressed her, pressing into him, rising to meet his touch. The first time they had kissed, she did not respond with protestations or false modesty, nor did she regard the moment as merely a casual exercise. Instead, she had stared into his eyes, sharing his desire, aware of the gift she was bestowing upon him, trusting him to respect her limits. But what had attracted him more was the way he felt whenever he was around her; comfortable and safe, unselfconscious. He found himself able to confide in her, to let her know his dreams and his fears, his secret hopes and his inner passions. He loved the contentment he felt by just being near her, the way holding her hand was like making love to her.

"How old were you when you got married?" he asked his grandfather.

The old man cocked an eyebrow and nibbled at his bottom lip.

"Same age as you are now."

He wasn't quite sure he wanted to get involved in this conversation, yet he sensed the boy was looking for some guidance or at least some reassurance. He took a breath.

"Why?"

"Just wondering."

The boy searched for a way to phrase his next question, unsure even of what the question was.

"I mean," he began, hoping the question would become apparent to one of them as he talked. "I mean, I've still got another year of college, still, so naturally, I'm not about to get married or anything, but . . . " But what? What was it that he wanted to know, needed to hear?

The old man knew. "Look, there's no such thing as the right time or the wrong time, only the right or wrong person. When you find the right person, you'll make the time fit. You've got lots of time, but the right person only comes along once in your life."

He had said his piece. Beside him, the boy nodded. Somehow the question had been asked and answered.

The old man rubbed his arms briskly, enjoying the tingling sensation as the friction warmed his skin against the chill night air. "Well," he said, "I'm turnin' in. See ya' in the mornin'." He started for the door, then turned back to the boy who still stood leaning against the the railing.

"Like I said before, I think she's a keeper."

A late snow was falling outside, defiantly challenging the coming spring. The ice was all but gone from the lake and huge wet flakes splattered on the open black water. The young couple had just come in from a walk to the dam. They peeled off their wet jackets and kicked off their boots. The melting snow had soaked through their coats, darkening the shoulders and backs of their sweaters. Their jeans clung to their thighs.

"We'd better get out of these wet clothes," the boy said. "I'll get us some towels."

"You just want to see me naked," she grinned at him mischievously.

He looked at her with feigned hurt and innocence. "I'm only concerned for your health. Besides, my grandparents are right next door." He would have liked to seen her body, though. Since that night a couple of months ago, when they had first made love, he had thought of little else.

"Excuses, excuses," she teased. She took a towel from the linen closet, then tossed him one. As she disappeared into her bedroom, she slipped her sweatshirt off over her head, treating him to a glimpse of white lace and soft flesh that inflamed him as much as if she had stood there nude. It took all of his self-control to retreat to his own room to change.

He was kneeling in front of the fireplace, stirring the flaming logs with a wrought iron poker, when she came back into the room. In fresh corduroy jeans and a thick cowl neck sweater, she was softness and warmth personified. She stood behind him and gently rubbed his damp hair with the towel that hung 'round his shoulders.

"That fire feels nice," she said. She had gotten a chill that a change of clothes and a vigorous towelling had been unable to chase away. The heat of the flames and a sudden memory of how it had felt when he had entered her for the first time now began to warm her. She let the towel fall and pressed against him, combing his thick locks with her fingers. He closed his eyes and leaned his head back against her belly.

"Marry me," he said.

"Oh sure," she chuckled deep in her throat. "You're just too lazy to dry your own hair."

He twisted around and took her hands in his, gently drawing her down to her knees beside him.

"I mean it. Marry me. Please."

His eyes searched her face, looking into her eyes, into her. She could feel his honesty, his love for her that went beyond mere words. She had hoped for this moment, dreamt of it. Now it was here. Her throat tightened and her eyes blurred and flooded. The last of the chill left her as she looked back into the eyes of the man who would be her husband.

"Yes," she whispered.

They were asleep on the couch when the old man and his wife came home. The boy was lying propped against a pillow, the girl beside him, her head and one hand on his chest. A book lay on the floor where it had fallen from the boy's grasp. Night had fallen while they slept and the darkened cottage was bathed in the bright orange glow of the embers shimmering in the fireplace.

"Should we wake them?" asked the boy's grandmother. Her sense of propriety was in conflict with her sense of romance.

"Naw, let' em be." The old man covered them with a blanket. "They're both dressed so no harm, no foul. Anyways, look at them. Do you want to wake them up?"

"No, I suppose not."

"Besides," he nudged his wife's hip with a knuckle and gave her his best leer. "Eh, eh?"

She slapped playfully at his hand. "You . . . ," she whispered reproachfully.

"C'mon. I won't tell 'em if you don't."

"What am I going to do with you?"

"I've got a few ideas."

She took his hand and led him toward the bedroom. "You're nothing but a dirty old man, aren't you?"

"You know it."

"May I have this dance?"

She looked up at the old man, standing stiffly, formally before her with his right hand outstretched, palm up. She smiled and slipped her hand into his.

"I would be honoured," she said with an exaggerated curtsey. She allowed him to lead her onto the dance floor. A 'Twist'-medley was just ending and couples were limping back to their tables, puffing for air and holding their sides. The soft trombones of Glenn Miller's "Moonlight Serenade" began to throb. The old man lightly cupped her right hand in his left, taking the weight of the long train that she held up off of the ground. He placed his right hand against the small of her back, making contact with the side of his thumb and wrist, careful not to soil the white satin of her wedding dress with the oil and sweat of his palm. She placed her left hand on his shoulder, her fingers reaching to the nape of his neck. The old man waited for the beat, then began to guide her skilfully around the floor. He was a graceful dancer and she easily followed his lead.

"You look very beautiful. Matter of fact, I can't say as I've ever seen a more beautiful bride," he said.

"This old thing? It's just something I threw on." She wore a satin and lace gown with a full-length sleeve and a heavily crinolined skirt. The key-hole neckline complimented the shape of her face and teasingly displayed a creamy teardrop of soft skin. Her rich chestnut hair was pulled back into a French braid and her veil was held in place by the same headpiece her mother had worn forty years earlier. Something old.

She realized even as she spoke that his compliment had not been an off-hand remark, but was an expression of a deeper sentiment, a way for the old man to declare the feelings he had for her. She smiled apologetically.

"Thank you." She squeezed his shoulder and he twirled her as if they both had taken flight, then danced in silence until the final chorus. As it began, the old man stepped away from her, holding her at arm's length. His steps lost a little of their fluidity.

"You'll take good care of him." It was spoken not so much as an assumption, as it was as a question, a plea. She was aware of how much her husband meant to the old man, but it hadn't occurred to her that he might worry in this way. Yet, here he was, seeking her assurance and she was overwhelmed by the tenderness of his concern.

"Don't worry. I will."

The song ended and she kissed his cheek.

It was well past midnight and the newlyweds were saying their goodbyes.

"Still no plans for a honeymoon?" the old man asked.

"Naw, all our money's going towards furniture and stuff." The couple would spend their first night as husband and wife at the local Holiday Inn but, although they each had taken a week off work, they had elected to use their savings to furnish and decorate their apartment rather than spend it on a honeymoon vacation.

The two men shook hands and the younger of the two felt something cold and hard pressed into his palm. He looked down at the key to the cottage then back up at his grandfather's wry smile.

"Try not to spend all your time fishin', eh," he advised with a broad wink.

They were relaxing on a blanket atop the granite dome overlooking the lake. The young man lay with his hands behind his head, chewing on a blade of grass while watching a soft white cloud drift lazily overhead. He had pulled his jeans back on, but had not yet bothered to do them up. The girl sat cross-legged beside him, an unbuttoned denim shirt her only clothing. She was idly plucking the petals from an ox-eye daisy. He loves me, he loves me not. He loves me.

"How did you find out about this place, anyway," she asked.

"My grandfather and I found it while we were hiking one day. We used to come up here a lot and just sit and look at the view. You can see just about the whole south end of the lake from up here. It's one of my favourite places."

She looked out at the blue water, the dark green pines and the emerald-gold of the new aspen leaves. "I can see why," she said quietly.

He squinted up at her. From this angle, she was backlit by the afternoon sun, her profile outlined with golden light. "The view's improving, too."

She caught his meaning and smiled, blushing. She was easily embarrassed by compliments.

"So," she said, trying change the subject, "What's the name of that bay out there?"

He pulled himself into a sitting position beside her. "Big Clear. And that's Big Black on the other side of the point, there."

"Where's Little Clear Bay, then?"

"Over the other side of the lake. You can just see the mouth of it off to the left of that big pine."

"How about Little Black?"

"There isn't one."

"Why don't they just call that one plain old Black Bay, then?" she asked.

"Don't know. My grandfather has a book with a map in it, though. It shows that Samuel de Champlain probably paddled across Big Black."

She looked out across the water and imagined she saw long birch-bark canoes full of natives with glistening black hair and shining, well-muscled bodies paddling alongside swarthy, bearded voyageurs, their red toques bright against the dark water and the green shore.

"What do you suppose he was looking for around here?"

"Little Black Bay."

She swatted his arm and he laughed. He got to his feet and began searching for his shoes.

"We'd better get heading back. It'll be getting dark soon," he said.

On the blanket, she leaned back, stretching her legs out luxuriously in front of her. The shirt she was wearing fell open and she arched her naked body towards the warmth of the late afternoon sun. She watched her husband as he hunted in the long grass for articles of their clothing and she thought about the past week.

It had been quite a honeymoon. They had made love in the boathouse and in the kitchen, on the dock beneath a blanket and in the lake beneath a quarter-moon. Although they had been intimate prior to being wed, she found the legitimacy of marriage had given freedom to her most carnal desires.

She watched as a bead of perspiration trickled its way down between her up-thrust breasts.

"Hey, Champlain," she said, her voice low and husky. "Why don't you explore your way over here?"

CHAPTER 11

The chapel had begun to fill up, people approaching the family to offer last minute words of support and comfort. Others lingered by the casket, still unable to believe the old man was dead.

After a few minutes the funeral director appeared and asked everyone to please take their seats. A heavy curtain was drawn then, separating the family from the rest of the mourners, providing them with a degree of privacy as they said their final goodbyes. The young man and his father took turns escorting the women to the casket then back to their seats where they wept in silence. Soon they had all made the last trip and the young man found himself alone with his father, looking down at the old man.

A million images and words unspooled in the young man's mind. Seasons chased one another, marking the changes brought about by the passing years. Smells of woodsmoke and boathouses, damp earth and frying bacon wafted up from his memory. Snatches of songs about cowboys and gunfighters, stampeding cattle and dusty wagon trains sung in a rich, soft tenor mixed with the whir of line sailing out from a spinning reel and the hushed gurgle of a topwater lure bubbling across the moonlit surface of a hidden bay. A coin slipped into a small child's hand ("Get yourself an ice cream"), or a cottage key given to an eager young honeymooner ("Don't spend all your time fishin' ").

Shake the hand of an honest man. Always look a man in the eye. Fifteen-two.

He looked at his grandfather's face, now, and smiled, not so much sad for his loss as happy and grateful for having had the experience of knowing him.

At the young man's side, his father fought back tears, surprised at the depth of his feelings of loss. Over the past few days, he had come to realize how the old man was the father-figure his own father had never been. The guidance and support and security he had received from the old man was so natural, it wasn't until it had been taken away that he realized how important it had been to him. Unexpectedly, he felt very alone and very lost.

The young man had noticed his father's uncharacteristic show of emotion and it disturbed him. Suddenly, he felt very protective of his father and he put a reassuring hand on his shoulder.

"You okay?"

"Yeah . . . fine." He offered the old man a silent thank you, then blinked away his tears and composed his expression to one he hoped conveyed strength and invulnerability. His father-in-law would have approved.

"We better go sit down," he said to his son. "The women are going to need us".

The minister, a pink little man with thin sandy hair, had not known the old man . He had gathered bits of information from the family and would weave these into his service. Now, he approached the lectern to the overture of a sombre hymn being squeezed out of the chapel organ by a blue-haired accompanist in a loud floral print dress. He reached into the side pocket of his rumpled blue suit coat and withdrew his notes. Placing them in front of him, he smoothed them with a sweep of his hand and signalled for the music to cease.

He began with a prayer and then moved into a description of life in heaven where pain and fear were unknown and the deceased would "dwell in the house of the Lord." The blue haired lady then wheezingly led the mourners through another hymn, most of them only mouthing the words. The young man couldn't help but think the old man would have preferred "Streets of Laredo" or "The Strawberry Roan." Maybe even "Bury Me Not On The Lone Prairie." The minister caught him chuckling at the thought and wondered what the hell could be so funny.

The hymn ended and they all sat down. The minister consulted his notes and then began to speak of the old man. He told of his devotion to his family, his generosity and sense of humour, his love of westerns and fishing. He spoke in generalities, taking the familys' word that these descriptions were accurate. But as he looked out at those assembled, he could see the nods and smiles. He knew that his words were conjuring up hundreds of memories of times spent with the old man out on a quiet lake, of his soft voice crooning a cowboy tune, or laughter at some now forgotten joke. A few bucks slipped into a pocket, ("Only a loan, pay me back when your luck changes"), not caring that it probably never would be.

He summed up with the Lord's Prayer and a couple of verses of "Amazing Grace" that made the young man's mother weep. It always did.

A long string of cars moved slowly towards the cemetery, their high beams burning into the cold grey gloom of an overcast afternoon. A pair of police cars, their red lights flashing, leapfrogged past one another, stopping traffic at the intersections until the procession had filed by.

Fourth in line, the young man rode in Stan's Cadillac with the other pallbearers, each silent and nervous. The only sound came from the wipers as they slapped intermittently at the freezing drizzle that spotted the windshield. They drove through the cemetery gate and followed a gravelled laneway to where a mound of freshly-excavated earth marked the grave site. The hole itself was covered with plywood and disguised with a mat of bright green carpet.

The pallbearers rolled the coffin out of the hearse, taking their places along the oaken bars that served as carrying handles. They took the weight of their burden and carried it carefully to the side of the grave, the smooth leather soles of their dress shoes slipping on the wet grass.

"Easy guys," the young man's father warned in a hoarse whisper. "If we drop him, he's gonna be pissed."

Across the coffin, the young man snorted. They eased the coffin onto the platform and stepped away to the shelter of several umbrellas. Droplets of rain beaded on the polished surface of the casket, the wood beneath glowing in spite of the dull light. The minister recited the final blessing and the service was over.

Ashes to ashes. Dust to dust.

People began moving away towards their cars with their shoulders hunched and their chins tucked inside their collars against the damp March chill.

The young man's grandmother stood staring, not at the coffin, but at the patch of ground beside her husband's grave. She felt strangely comforted looking at the place where, one day, she would again lay beside him.

The mourners were gathered in small pockets around the young man's parent's house, balancing paper plates and Styrofoam coffee cups. The dining room table sagged beneath platters of crustless sandwiches of ham and pickle, peanut butter and banana, egg salad and mystery cold meat, each cut into fingers or dainty triangles or rolled into colourful pinwheels. Trays of cookies and cakes, tarts and squares sat temptingly alongside veggies and dip. The women constantly flitted between the dining room and the kitchen, rearranging and restocking the table as the food was rapidly consumed. The men stood around, looking uncomfortable in suits and ties and stockinged feet, talking about mileage and overpaid athletes. "Ottawa and back on one tank, pretty good." "For two million a year he should be able to hit the goddamned ball blindfolded." Every now and again, one would relate an anecdote about the old man and they would laugh and sip their coffee and stare straight ahead, uneasily.

People fussed around the young man's grandmother until she couldn't stand it any longer. She had already drunk three cups of over-sweetened tea, and two more were going cold on the table beside her. A plate of goodies sat untouched in her lap. Finally, she got up and pulled her grandson aside.

"Come with me," she said and led him to the room that was now her only home. She closed the door behind him and sat down on the edge of the bed. The room had been the young man's when he had still lived at home and it threw him a little to see flowered wallpaper and white wicker furniture where a short time ago, rock posters and cinder block-and-plywood bookshelves had been. His grandmother patted the bed and he sat down beside her.

"I just needed some peace and quiet," she sighed. "And I wanted to talk to you. You know your grandfather thought the world of you?" The young man nodded. "I know he'd want you to have something to remember him by. Is there anything special you would like to have? His good watch, maybe?"

The young man thought for a moment. "Could I have his army medals?"

The old man had first shown him the two medals years before, opening the flat white boxes to reveal the metal discs and the coloured ribbons that lay inside on beds of cotton wool. The boy had felt the cold surfaces, the relief figures like braille beneath his fingertips.

He'd lifted the 1939-45 War Medal from its box, holding it by it's red, blue and white striped ribbon.

"They gave that one to everybody who was in the service during the war," the old man had told him. The boy returned it to its box and then laid the other medal out in his hand. This one was embossed with the Canadian Coat of Arms on one side and a parade of marching servicemen and women on the other. A ribbon of dark green, navy blue and blood red was clasped by a silver bar stamped with a maple leaf.

"That one was given to everyone who volunteered." The old man touched the leaf. "They added this for the one's who volunteered to go overseas. Not everybody did." The boy had studied the conscription crisis in school. He was proud his grandfather hadn't been a zombie.

The old man put the lids back on the boxes and tucked them back into their hiding place in his sock drawer. "They're not for anything special," the old man said apologetically. "Lots of guys got them."

They might not have meant much to the old man, but to the boy, they were badges of bravery and pride and virtue, emblematic of the triumph of good over evil, symbolic of the courage of his nation and an inherited obligation to uphold these values, a modern-day extension of the code of the cowboy.

His grandmother, although unaware of the importance of the medals to the young man agreed to his request.

"I don't think they're worth much," she said. "But of course, if you want them, you can have them. Is there anything else you would like?"

The young man thought again, searching his mind for a momento that defined his relationship with the old man. It came to him in a flash; a token of the best times they had spent together, all their most perfect moments.

"His tackle box, the green steel one. I'd like to have it if I could."

"His tackle box?" At first she wondered what on earth he would want with that rusty old thing. Then, slowly, pictures began to form in her mind; the small boy carrying the heavy box in both hands; the way he would inhale while opening it, breathing in the escaping odours as though they were the most delicious narcotic in the world.

"The tackle box," she agreed, patting him on the hand. "Well," she got up, "We should be getting back before they miss us and send out the dogs." She drew a deep breath and opened the door.

She was sitting in a corner, tensed against the well-meaning sympathy that flooded over her, smothering her. Her grandson appeared then, a china cup and saucer in his hand.

"Here, Nana, I brought you some tea," he said.

Oh God, she thought, *Not more tea.*

"Thank you," she said, smiling weakly. She raised the cup to her lips and the smell of rum rose to her on the steam. She sipped and felt a heat that was not entirely from the tea calming her, untying the knots in her shoulders. She drank again, more deeply, and closed her eyes.

"How's the tea?" the young man asked, his eyes glinting with mischief.

"Fine, dear, just fine." She drained the cup and handed it to him. "May I have another?"

He smiled and headed for the kitchen.

* * *

It was a little late in the morning for the fishing to be really any good. From the mouth of the bay, the old man and the boy could hear the roar and the whine of the glittering speedboats as they began tearing up and down the lake.

"Goddamned terrorists," spat the old man as he flipped a yellow plastic grub sidearm into the shadow of a dead-fallen cedar. Beside him the young man grinned.

"So you're really goin' south for the winter this year, eh?" the boy asked.

"Yep, your grandmother said if we spent one more winter frozen in up here, she was gonna leave me. So after a lot of thought, I agreed to get a trailer down in Florida. Anyways, there's supposed to be decent fishing down around there."

The old man had retired two years before and he and his wife gave up their apartment and moved into the cottage to live full-time. Two long winters of snowy isolation and frequent power outages had been enough for his wife and, if truth be known, the novelty had worn off for the old man as well. When they had driven down to Florida the previous February to visit friends, they had fallen in love with the lifestyle of the retirement park. The forty foot trailer with it's double tip-outs was bigger than their first home and twice as comfortable . There were neighbours, dances, activities and, most importantly, warmth. The old man had noticed that the older he got, the deeper the cold seeped into his bones. When he was younger, he had been impervious to the cold, but now it stiffened his fingers and got his knees to aching. A winter in the sun seemed quite appealing these days.

"We'll go down after Thanksgiving and come back for a few days at Christmas," the old man explained. "Then we'll head back down until the end of April. We'll have to come back then in time to do our taxes."

He looked over at his grandson. The young man was staring ahead, studying the tip of his fishing rod.

"We're even thinking of selling the cottage."

The young man stiffened, but said nothing.

The old man went on, almost apologetic. "The place is a lot to take care of. The taxes up here are killers, too. The lake's so busy now that you can't even go for a nice boat ride on the weekend," A passing Seaflea punctuated his last observation with a buzzing exclamation point. "Besides, everybody's selling off. Ed and Marion, Stan. It's getting lonely up here during the week."

The young man nodded. Now that he was married with a life of his own, he couldn't find the time to come up as much as he would have liked. Another ski boat blasted past the mouth of the bay, it's wake sloshing in to rock their small fishing boat. On the shore of the quiet, hidden bay, flourescent orange survey ribbons fluttered from the trees, marking a dozen or so future building lots. Maybe it was time to sell, while the memories were still good.

"Remember the time I got my new Dardevil snagged in this bay and you had to dive in and get it?" the young man asked.

The old man smiled and nodded. "You just about became a boat anchor that day." The young man still had not commented on the idea of selling the cottage. The old man flipped the grub back towards cover and began to retrieve it.

The young man cast out his own lure but let it sink to the bottom as he spoke. "Maybe the cottage has outlived it's purpose; you know. I mean, we enjoyed it when we could all get together. We had a lot of good times here. But things are changing. We don't have the time to spend up here and you and Nana get lonely just the two of you. I guess maybe it is time to sell."

The old man was relieved that the boy understood. He was a man who usually made up his own mind and to hell with what anyone else thought. But from the moment he and his wife began to discuss selling the cottage, the reaction of the young man preyed on his mind. He was glad his grandson did not resent him for his decision.

"Anyway," the young man went on, "It's about the people, not the place so much. We've all gotten older. We've all changed. Lately, it seems there are no new memories, just attempts to recreate old ones and since none of us are who we used to be, it never works out. The good times were of their time, they needed us to be who we were, when we were. Memories just happen, we can't manufacture them. Maybe selling the cottage is the only way to protect those memories that we have."

"That's the way I had it figured," the old man said. "It's just a building." . He knew as well as the boy that it was much more than just a building, that it was the place where grandfather and grandson had always been best able to connect. But he also knew that the decision was inevitable and he was glad the boy accepted it, even going so far as to help with the rationalization. "When did you get so smart, anyways?"

The young man tugged at his line, the tip of his rod bowing down toward the water. *Shit.* "I don't know about getting smart. I think I'm snagged again," he said sheepishly.

Marjorie's daughter, the cottage real estate queen, showed the young couple around the cottage. It was a perfect fall day, crisp and clear, the sharp tang of wood smoke on the air. Marjorie's daughter could not have been more pleased. On days like this, cottages practically sold themselves, especially to idealistic yuppies seeking to escape the city.

The couple, in their early thirties, were quintessential yuppies. Today, he was wearing soft, wide-wale corduroys, pressed and pleated and supported with a belt of braided leather. A pale-teal, knitted sweater, its shawl collar adorned with wooden toggle buttons, was pulled over a starched denim shirt with a button-down collar. On his feet he wore a pair of two hundred dollar hiking boots, their dark brown uppers oiled and pristine, showing not so much as a scuff mark. He felt that this was the proper attire for one to wear when one was roughing it.

She wore a denim skirt that reached midway down her calf and, beneath an oversized cable knit sweater, a dainty blouse decorated with a delicate floral pattern was buttoned to the neck, its lace trimmed collar set off by a choker of perfect pearls. Her tan penny loafers held pesos from their recent trip to Mexico. Underneath, she wore a silk teddy that made her feel positively wicked.

He was Richard, a stockbroker who made more money in a year than his foundry-worker father had made in his lifetime.

She was Kathryn, a corporate lawyer from a good corporate family.

In front of waiters, real estate agents, hired help and close family and friends, they addressed one another as "Richard" and "Kathryn." But in private, swept up in the throes of unbridled passion, they referred to one another as . . . "Richard" and "Kathryn"

The product of one of these passionate moments now explored about the lot. The little boy was four going on thirty-seven. He had the same thick blonde hair and pale blue eyes as both his parents. Marjorie's daughter had immediately thought of an article she had recently read about selective breeding. Aside from the fact he was wearing tiny Levi's, he was a miniature clone of his father.

Richard had wanted to name his son "Miles" after Miles Davis, the great jazz trumpeter that Richard liked to pretend he understood. Kathryn was partial to "Emerson" after Ralph Waldo Emerson (There was no way on earth she was going to call her son "Ralph" or "Waldo").

Eventually the settled on "Ethan", a favourite character on their favourite television show (Kathryn had also suggested "Scout", but Richard, never having read "To Kill a Mockingbird," thought she meant to name their child after Tonto's horse and so ended that discussion).

Anyway, Ethan was along today only because it was the nanny's day off.

They had pulled up that morning in their Jeep Grand Cherokee and immediately began gushing over the property, their primary adjectives being "quaint" and "rustic". *Of course it's rustic,* thought Marjorie's daughter, *You're in the goddamned woods!* The boathouse was "wonderful", the dock was "marvellous" and the view was "simply grand." Richard had even gone so far as to describe the kitchen as "a paradigm of simple efficiency."

Marjorie's daughter followed them around, maintaining her smile by imagining the joy she would receive by choking the living shit out of both of them. She was even beginning to hate cute little Ethan.

It took over four hours, but Richard and Kathryn finally agreed to the asking price.

"What do you want done with these life jackets?" The young man held up an armful of faded orange keyhole vests.

"Might as well leave 'em here. I don't have room in the trailer to store them."

"Same with the extra gas cans?"

"Yeah, I guess so."

They were cleaning out the cottage and the boathouse, removing things the old man wanted to keep, leaving for the new occupants those things that he could no longer use. The activity had put him in a dark mood that wasn't made any better by the cold November sky.

The glorious vibrancy of autumn had given way to a grey-brown gloom not yet softened by the pure white slumber of winter. November smelled of decay and death. Those animals that slept until spring were deep in their burrows. The birds that migrated south to sun themselves in warmer climes had flown, taking their sweet song with them. Any life that remained was silent and resolute, steeling for the deprivations the coming winter would bring.

For nearly sixty-five years, the old man had faced the winter with determination. Yet in another week, he would join the snow-birds and fly south to wait for spring to return with it's warmth and life.

"I don't know. Maybe it was a mistake to sell."

The old man had been depressed ever since the real estate deal had gone through. The sale had saddened him, of course. He was after all, parting with something that had been a very significant part of his life. But the sale had also frightened him. He would be discussing the trailer that awaited him in the Florida sunshine when, from out of nowhere, his belly would tighten, the fire inside turning to ice. His lungs would freeze in terror, unable to neither draw breath nor expel it. Sweat would trickle down his back and his bowels would grow weak with dread. Instead of looking forward to an idyllic retirement, far from the cold of winter, he felt instead like a man rushing headlong towards a dark abyss, casting aside his worldly possessions, living a transient life as a way of prolonging a losing game of hide-and-seek against death itself. By selling the cottage and fleeing south, he was severing his bonds to all that he had known to be safe and familiar. He became like a man adrift at sea, clinging desperately to life while waiting for the sharks he knew would soon come.

"You'll have fun in Florida. No snow, no ice, no cold wind." The young man tried hard to sound reassuring, yet he too felt his grandfather slipping away. He hadn't had the same premonitions that terrorized the old man. Instead, with the cottage gone, he felt that they were losing perhaps their most important touchstone, the common ground where the years would magically melt away and he would once again be six years old and his grandfather would once again be his hero, his saviour. Now, suddenly, he was a young man out on his own, drifting away from the touchstone in one direction while his grandfather drifted away in another.

The old man finished hanging the paddles on their nails and turned around, having one last look at the interior of the boat-house. He breathed in one last time the odours; the earthy scent of old wood, the penetrating pungency of gasoline and oil, the clean sweetness of the lake water that lapped gently a couple of feet below the floorboards; the musty odour of mice and old canvas. He reached out and thumped a wall stud with the side of his fist. *Still solid,* he thought. *We built 'er to last a lifetime.* A lifetime.

The young man waited at the door with an armload of fishing rods.

"Ready to go?" he asked the old man softly.

The old man picked up his battered steel tackle box, surprised at it's weight. He brushed a dried, dead leaf from its scarred, green lid. He suddenly wondered if he would be around next summer to use it. *Oh God, no I'm not ready. Not yet.*

"Papa?"

"Yeah . . . I'm ready."

They walked out, locking the latch behind them.

The old man celebrated his sixty-fifth birthday with is wife and six other couples they had met only the week before. He had danced and drank and opened their gag gifts, forcing laughter at juvenile novelties these strangers had given him. He wore a silly hat with an elastic under his chin and his left cheek was smudged with six goodwill kisses in six different shades of lipstick. It was well past eleven when the last guest finally left.

He and his wife began to straighten up the trailer, putting the glasses in the sink to soak, checking the cushions on the sofa for stray embers from the dozens of cigarettes that had been smoked that night. She opened the windows to allow the fresh air to clear away the smoke.

"I'm going to bed," she said.

"Okay".

"Are you coming?," she placed a hand on his shoulder.

"I'm gonna stay up for a little while. I'll be along in a bit".

"Okay." There was concern in her voice. "Try not to stay up too late".

He poured himself a drink and went out onto the patio. A warm breeze blew in off the Gulf. He sat down in a plastic lawn chair and pulled off the party hat he had been wearing all evening. The elastic had left a red line around his throat. "HAPPY 65TH" was emblazoned across the front.

"Happy 65th. Happy 65th my ass.". He crumpled the hat in his fist and took a long gulp from his glass, grimacing as the rye burned the back of his throat.

Sixty-five.

His father had been sixty-five when he died. Years of spray-painting cars without the protection of a mask had ruined his lungs. He frequently suffered coughing spells so severe that he would rupture blood vessels and then he would spit blood. It had been during one such attack that his heart finally gave out. He died the next day, exactly eight months past his sixty-fifth birthday.

Alex had been sitting at home, asleep in his favourite chair, three months past his sixty-fifth, when an aneurysm took his life. His wife found him two hours later when she came in from shopping.

Lately, they had been visiting the old man in his dreams. They would not speak, only hover on the periphery of whatever else was taking place, silently reminding him of his own mortality. Each time he saw them, he would awaken with an uneasiness, a sense of foreboding that would haunt him for the rest of the day.

They had last appeared two nights before. The memory of it now made the old man's scalp prickle. He had dreamt of a dance, of waltzing dizzily around the floor, his wife encircled in his arms. They came then, standing amongst the crowd surrounding the dance floor. The old man saw them and although he still held his wife, he felt as though he was being pulled away, her face becoming less and less distinct behind a sudden wall of mist. He watched as a portal opened behind the two visitors and they both began to slide through. Then something happened that had never happened before. They turned to him and made silent contact. Alex reached out his right hand, palm up, his fingers lightly curled. *Take my hand*, the gesture seemed to say. *Come with us*. Beside him, their father smiled and nodded. They disappeared as the portal closed. The old man, startled awake, found himself lying wrapped in sweat-soaked sheets, eyes wide with fright searching the darkened ceiling for a reference point, greedily gulping down lungfuls of air.

Sitting outside the trailer, the old man shivered in spite of the warm night air and gooseflesh textured his arms. He took a swallow from the drink in his hand and set the glass down on the plastic table at his side.

He had taken the dream as a premonition of his own death. He was not normally a superstitious man, but it had left him feeling as though he was predestined to die at the same age as his father and his brother. Their most recent visit had only reinforced his fate.

He looked out at the trailer park. Christmas was only two weeks away and plastic snowmen and coloured lights tried valiantly to present a yuletide spirit amongst the tropical shrubbery and the pink flamingoes. He slumped deeper into the lawn chair and sighed. *I wonder if it's snowing back home*, he thought as he drifted off to sleep.

The St. Patrick's Day dance had been a great success. The old man had danced with all the ladies and had sung along with all the Irish songs, his rich voice affecting a slight Gaelic lilt. He sang along with "When Irish Eyes Are Smiling," "My Wild Irish Rose," and even allowed a tear or two at "Danny Boy." He drank beer and rye, both shaded green for the occasion, and speculated at what colour his piss would be in the morning. The only drawback was the overcooked corned beef and cabbage he had eaten for dinner. It had given him a fierce case of indigestion.

"Al and Doris want us to go back to their trailer for cards," his wife said.

He gulped hard, swallowing air, trying unsuccessfully to get under the gas bubble that was causing his distress. The pain of it radiated across his chest and back and even into his shoulders and arms.

"Okay, but I'm gonna go back to our place first for a couple of minutes." He thought that maybe a good dump would make him feel better, but he didn't want to pollute someone else's trailer. "I'll meet you there." He winced at a fresh stab of pain.

She reached out and touched his arm. "Are you alright?"

"Yeah, I'm fine. Just don't let me eat corned beef again, okay," He smiled to put her mind at ease. "I'll be right along." He kissed her lightly and headed for the trailer, his green plastic derby cocked jauntily over one eyebrow.

Inside he was hit by another spasm. "Geezus, what was in that dinner?" He belched without relief. Picking up one of his wife's tabloids, he made his way into the bathroom and sat down.

He was halfway through a story of a woman who thought her cat was the reincarnation of Elvis when suddenly a pain worse than anything he had ever known took away his breath. A cold wave of nausea swept over him. The magazine twisted and crumpled in his hands. The paroxysm sent him pitching from the toilet onto his hands and knees. He curled into a tight ball on the floor until the pain ebbed slightly and he rolled onto his side, coughing. He felt ridiculous and vulnerable with his pants around his knees and he laughed weakly to himself. He figured it was bad enough to go without his boots on, but he'd be damned if they'd find him with his pants around his ankles. He struggled until they were up over his hips. He slumped back against the wall and looked at himself in the mirror on the back of the bathroom door. His colour was not good, his face a pale grey. Shiny circles under his eyes were the colour of bruises. Sweat beaded in icy drops across his forehead. The pain seized him again, his chest tightening in a knot of unrelenting iron. He bit his lower lip until the skin broke and blood trickled down his chin, his eyes squeezing against the agony until tears ran down his cheeks. When at last he was again able to opened his eyes, his father and Alex stood in the mirror, looking down at him. His father smiled, kindly, invitingly. Again, Alex reached out to him. The pain burst free from his chest, leaving a comforting warmth which flooded his body with a strange calm. The room suddenly seemed unusually large and bright.

He slipped his hand into his brother's and he was gone.

It was seven o'clock on a Sunday morning when he awoke to the ringing of the phone. . . .

CHAPTER 12

The young man's father stood staring through the window that separated the hospital nursery from the hallway. On the other side of the glass, his grandson lay in a clear plastic bassinette, swaddled in a white flannel blanket. The wizened little face glared in curious anger at the other squalling infants that surrounded him, his eyes a glittering cobalt blue. A cock's comb of fine blonde hair rose from the top of his small head. His rose petal bottom lip worked in and out, sucking against a non-existent nipple. A tiny fist, the thumb tucked inside the fingers, punched out from under the blanket and began to jerkily wave about.

At the window, the young man's father grinned at the sight. He lightly tapped on the glass with a fingertip and was rewarded immediately with a smile. He knew it was actually just a timely gas bubble, but he lied to himself that it was a smile just the same.

Beside him, his wife waggled her fingers at the baby boy.

"Isn't he cute," she declared. "Look at his little fingers."

Her husband could only smile and stare.

"He's got your chin, I think," his wife went on, "and your mouth."

"He's got your dad's nose," he said to his wife.

She looked closely and realized her husband was right. She thought then of her father, dead now almost six years. He would have loved this moment, would have made a wonderful great-grandfather.

Her husband read her silence.

"Should we head down to the room and give them the present I got for the little guy?" he asked.

He had gone out that morning by himself, leaving his wife to sleep late. He wanted to get something special for his grandson, something from him and him alone.

He walked through toy stores and book stores, shops full of baby clothes and commemorative knick-knacks. Nothing seemed quite right, nothing said what he wanted to say.

Then it came to him. Perfect. It would be perfect.

"It" was a small black fielder's glove, about half the size of a regulation baseball mitt. It smelled of leather and oil and summer. As he held it up to his face, he saw himself teaching his grandson to catch, the small boy holding the glove out awaiting the throw, he lobbing the ball underhand, aiming carefully for the pocket. Later, he would teach him to throw, then hit and bunt. They would go together to munch peanuts and hotdogs at the ballpark while he pointed out to his grandson the intricacies of the game. Later, he would sit on sun-baked wooden bleachers and cheer as the young short-stop ranged deep into the hole to scoop a sizzling ground ball, then pivoting and getting the runner by a step at first. He began to imagine himself at Tiger Stadium, or maybe Fenway. His grandson, tall and strong, would lope out of the dugout, search the stands until he found his grandfather's face and gave him a little wave. *Glad you're here.*

"A baseball glove? Isn't he a little young?" his wife had exclaimed when he brought it home.

"He'll grow into it."

"Well, I know, but . . . Oh for Pete's sake," she just shook her head. Her own father would probably have bought the baby a cowboy hat and toy six-shooter. Or a fishing rod. *What was it with men and boys?*, she wondered.

His daughter-in-law looked tired, but happy, his son tired and overwhelmed.

After a little while, a nurse wheeled his grandson into the room. Immediately his wife and daughter-in-law took charge of the infant, cuddling him, pampering him, oohing and aahing over his every little move. Finally, his son picked up the little guy. He carried him over and handed him to the proud new grandfather. For the first time, he held his grandson in his arms.

* * *

The young man stood hand in hand with his son, looking down at the dark granite headstone.

"That's your papa, right?" The boy's four year old mind was just beginning to understand relationships.

"That's right."

"He's dead, right?"

The young man smiled at the innocence of the question.

"Yep. He died before you were born."

The little boy thought of his own grandfather.

"Did you use'ta play ball together?" he asked.

"We use to go fishing together."

"Like we are," the boy cried happily. He had gotten a fishing pole a few weeks earlier for his birthday. Today, his father was taking him to a friend's cottage to try it out.

"That's right, just like we are."

He had stopped at the cemetery on the way north, the pretense being to check the small flower bed that adorned his grandfather's grave. Once there, he and his young son got out of the car. Somehow, his wife sensed that what had brought them here today did not involve her but had only to do with her husband, her son and the old man. She stayed in the car, not wanting to intrude.

The young man plucked a couple of weeds and pinched a few spent blossoms from the marigolds. He seemed to be searching for the best way to do what he had to do. Finally, he nudged his son.

"Here, I got a little present for you." He reached into his pocket and withdrew a thin, cellophane-covered box. He handed it to his son.

The boy looked at the tear-drop-shaped spoon, the red and white enamelled swirl, the silvered treble hook. He looked up at his father.

"It's a Dardevil," the young man said. "The best bass spoon ever."